About the Author

Rebecca is the sole parent to three awesome children, two of whom are now adults. She lives in West Sussex with her youngest daughter and the family dog. Having spent many years working with children in schools and sadly witnessing the daily struggles that these young people endure, Rebecca is amazed at what they take in their stride. Although working from home during the pandemic, Rebecca was inspired to use the opportunity to write *Minor Perception* in her snatches of free time.

Minor Perception: Summer Class

Rebecca Skinner

Minor Perception: Summer Class

Olympia Publishers
London

www.olympiapublishers.com
OLYMPIA PAPERBACK EDITION

A CIP catalogue record for this title is
available from the British Library.

ISBN: 978-1-80074-737-1

This is a work of fiction.
Names, characters, places and incidents originate from the writer's
imagination. Any resemblance to actual persons, living or dead, is
purely coincidental.

First Published in 2023

Olympia Publishers
Tallis House
2 Tallis Street
London
EC4Y 0AB

Printed in Great Britain

Dedication

I dedicate this book to my children and also to all those single parents who do it all alone.

Acknowledgements

Thank you so much for all the encouragement from my friends and family who believed in me when I started saying I wanted to write a book. Especially my mum, Rosemary; my sisters, Abigail and Naomi; my Auntie Priscilla; and my amazing friends, especially Jannine, Nikki and Sara who all took the time to read sections of the book and give me constructive feedback.

Author's Note

Working in a school has allowed me the opportunity to share the manuscript of Minor Perception with a few of the students I worked with in Year 8 and Year 9.

I did not disclose the fact that I was the author to them, instead telling them only that I knew of the publishers and had been given access to the story. We read and analysed the text and I asked them to write an honest review of what they thought.

We did not read to the end, so the students found themselves left in suspense, awaiting the publication date.

Minor Perception starts out as a story about a family of three who each struggle with their own problems. The book possesses an element of mystery, leaving many elements up to the reader's imagination. The book feels slow paced at first and there are many characters to keep track of but it still made for an entertaining read. 7.5/10

Freddie Lawrence Year 9. Age 14.

Minor Perception is a dramatic novel showing the lives of children just before Covid-19. I definitely want to carry on with this book, it's really good, I want to know more about each character's story. I like the part about the day the children go back to school because they get to see all their friends again. I will give this book a rating of 7/10.

Dylan Shrubb Year 8. Age 12.

Minor Perception makes me think the mum, Laura, has a drug problem and this makes me feel sad for the characters of Holly and Poppy. The book touches on so many issues that kids have to deal with and makes the reader have to use their own imagination. Otterlie, in the book, has anger issues too.
    Scarlett Brazil Year 9. Age 14.

Minor Perception is about all types of drama, set just before Covid-19 hits. It makes me want to know what happens next because there are lots of different issues going on. I liked all of the book in general. There was nothing I didn't like. I recommend it to everyone my age.
    Charlie Broadbridge Year 8. Age 13.

This book is decent. It shows issues that children face such as bullying, meanness, addiction and death. I liked the storylines but found the idea of addiction offending as I think drugs are bad. I would recommend Minor Perception to others. 7.9/10
    Billy Sewell Year 9. Age 14.

This kept me entertained throughout the book. I would have liked more scary moments that would make me not want to put it down. But it was a good book for age 11+. 7/10
    Max Metcalfe Year 9. Age 14.

Even though I have only read the first two chapters, I think the book is about real life in a way. Like Holly being bullied at school and the mum, Laura, being widowed and having to look after her kids alone. I am looking forward to reading the rest of the story.
    Charlie Year 9. Age 13.

Minor Perception tells the audience about issues such as bullying and drugs without actually saying it. The words are written between the lines. I liked the book because it was good.

Alfie Barrett Year 9. Age 14.

I like Minor Perception because it is through the eyes of a ten-year-old that is going through grief. I also like it because the main characters change throughout the book. It has a good moral that is – Don't be mean to people because you don't know what is going on at home. Therefore, I would rate it 8/10.

Jason Langridge Year 9. Age 14.

This book is about real events that could happen to children. It is set in Covid-19 times through the eyes of ten year olds. I like that it is actually realistic and although there was a lot going on, I could keep up with the plot. I would recommend Minor Perception to others because I found it interesting. 8.2/10

Oliver Heathorn Year 9. Age 14.

The book, Minor Perception, is about describing the world through the eyes of a 10-year-old. It also describes the problems in life. I liked the book because it is quite realistic and because it shows issues that children have to deal with in their daily lives. Therefore, my overall opinion of Minor Perception is that I think that it is an engaging book and I definitely recommend it to others.

Max Hopwood Year 9. Age 13

Chapter 1

Holly

I woke up with a jump, breathlessly laying still for a few seconds to calm myself. The sheet was sticking to me; my legs and neck damp with sweat. It was so unbearably hot and muggy in my bed. The stifling room abruptly lit up as the lightning flashed through the brightly coloured, polka dot curtains. I almost screamed as the door flew open followed by an extremely loud clap of thunder. Taking a deep breath, I let out a sigh and whispered to Poppy, my sister, to stop standing in my doorway and gestured to her to come and sit on my bed. Nothing to be scared of, I told myself – just a thunderstorm.

Although she was six years older than me, I knew Poppy was terrified of storms and, for the first time in a long time, she seemed young and vulnerable instead of the distant, moody sister she had become lately, always ready to argue with Mum and regularly slamming doors angrily on her way out of the house.

'I love you, Holly,' she murmured to me as she threw my crumpled sheet on the floor and then lay down next to me, our long, chestnut brown, sweaty hair touching. 'Don't ever grow up, stay my beautiful little, innocent sister forever.'

As we lay there trying not to touch too much in the sticky heat, I wondered what she had meant. I was going to be turning ten in two days' time (double figures, finally!) and I had to go back to school on my birthday, which did suck a bit but it also meant I would get sung to in assembly. My new teacher, Mrs Redleigh, was rumoured to bring in cakes to celebrate birthdays. Hopefully mine wouldn't be forgotten as it would be the first day back of the new school year…

When Holly woke up the next morning there was a smell of fresh rain coming through her open sash window, the storm during the night had brought much needed respite from the previous week of scorching, humid, muggy days. Poppy had gone from her position in the bed, although she could be heard clattering around in the bathroom. Holly quickly threw on her clothes, blue denim shorts and a sequinned t-shirt; crumpled and in a pile from yesterday, and yawning, ran downstairs.

Laura, her mother, was sitting on a bar stool with her head in her arms resting her forehead on the cool marble surface of the kitchen island, her short mousy hair was standing up in unkempt tufts and her glasses were precariously hanging from one ear. After kissing her mum on the head, Holly walked to the large American style, mint green fridge, opened both doors and groaned audibly.

Once again it was practically empty. Not really fancying the mouldy bread, foul smelling milk or the half bottle of wine that was staring back at her, Holly knew it would be down to her to order the online shopping again that morning. Happy last day of being nine and happy last day of the summer holidays, she thought to herself.

Laura opened her eyes and sat up. She subconsciously straightened her tortoiseshell designer frames and then smiled without using her eyes. Her voice was flat as she spoke, 'Morning, gorgeous daughter. I know, I know, I was going to go shopping last night but I got distracted with the old photo albums of your dad. Sorry, darling. Here's my card, order whatever we need plus lots of yummy treats for your lunch boxes at school. Whatever would we do without our Holly. My baby is turning ten…'

As Laura walked dejectedly out of the room and up the stairs, Holly pretended to ignore the gentle snivels that her mum was trying to mask. She heard Poppy shout something mean, aimed at her mother, from upstairs and the sound of a banging door vibrated violently through the house. Family life had been so much better when Poppy had helped keep their mum happy, before her sister had started hanging out with these new "friends" of hers. The dark red car was already waiting outside the gate at the end of the drive so Holly knew her sister wouldn't be hanging around that morning to help comfort their mother or to order the food.

Once she had finished the food shopping order, booked the time slot and put the iPad back on her mum's charger, Holly went back upstairs. It was colder today and she needed a hoodie. Her mum was just coming out of her private en-suite. She sniffed a few times, checked her nose in the landing mirror and then turned and smiled, much more convincingly, at her youngest daughter. Her chin length hair was no longer looking lank and straggly. Instead it was washed and styled. Her eyes looked bright again and the stress had drained from her face which was now perfectly made up and she was actually dressed for the first time in two days! Plastering a smile on her own face, Holly walked into the open arms for a big, loving mum squeeze. 'Don't know what I'm going to do with that sister of yours.' Laura sighed. 'Oh well, let's go out, treat ourselves to a late breakfast and then I'll take you shopping for your birthday cake. Plus, I'm feeling like it's a spending day so let's go and get all new stuff for your pencil case for Year Five and have a pedicure to celebrate!'

Smiling genuinely back at her mum, Holly could feel the anxious, wobbly feeling leaving her stomach. Maybe today would turn out all right after all. Happy, mumsy mum was back. On impulse, she ran and gave her another big hug. When her mum was happy, Holly felt that the world was a safer, less daunting, place.

For Holly, the day passed in a contented blur of quality bonding time with her mum. Shopping, laughing, pampering and lots of delicious treats, especially the sample mint cake they had tried, the refreshing taste lingering on the roof of her mouth. When Holly asked her mum why it was called the roof of her mouth and not the ceiling, her mum had just laughed out loud and shrugged. Laura seemed back on top form, chattering away about how well work was going, describing the wedding she had catered for where the groom had fallen into the pool, almost pulling his new mother-in-law in with him. Although Holly had heard the story before she laughed anyway. Her mum ran her own company, Catering for Kicks, and both Poppy and Holly were often rolling around in stitches at their mum's tales of the chaos that regularly occurred at the events. Generally, it seemed that the posher, and however well planned, the occasion – the worse people behaved.

Although Laura vanished a few times to the toilet throughout the day, often coming back sniffing and playing with her nose, Holly didn't think it was because she was upset. Even when Poppy sent a rude response to her mother's text message after Laura had inquired if she was all right, Laura just sighed and turned her attention back to her youngest daughter.

Later that evening, Holly spread all her new purchases out onto her bedroom floor. Her mum had gone overboard as usual; funky new stationery, a lunchbox with glittery shoulder strap, gorgeous patent school shoes, new shirts and socks, three new autumnal outfits, nail varnish and her most favourite item; a large, fluffy, red rucksack. The new clothes were so cool and Holly had felt ever so grown up at the time, getting them from the adult section of the store. Most of the children's range had seemed too small and nothing had fit her properly, so they'd tried on everything in an adult size ten-twelve. Laura had said it was because Holly was so tall and pretty but, now though, Holly felt the anxious butterflies flutter in her stomach, worries that when she went back to school some of the others in her class, children she had not even thought about for the last six weeks, would start up the snide comments again and call her "Hippo Holly". Remembering what her two best friends, Louise and Otterlie, had said to her, Holly let her worry turn to determined rage – she wouldn't let anyone be nasty this year. The three of them were going to take on the world!

The sound of singing woke Holly on the Fourth of September. Before she had even opened her eyes, she smiled to herself as the early morning realisation that it was her birthday spread through her body, making her feel all warm and tingly – today was going to be another good day.

Laura and Poppy burst into her room warbling the Happy Birthday song and laughing as they both pushed to be the first to sit on the bed. Laura held out a cake with ten candles burning brightly in the semi-darkness of the room. 'Happy birthday to my favourite ten-year-old daughter! Close your eyes and make a wish.'

'Thanks, Mum,' Holly replied. She glanced at Poppy who looked a bit worse for wear this morning. There seemed to be the shadow of a bruise on her neck and jaw. She was dressed already too, jeans, a long sleeve top and an oversized denim jacket, which made Holly feel hot just looking at her.

Holly felt the worry about her sister begin its squirmy sensation in her stomach. 'I wish... I wish that we can all have a lovely day out as a family, all three of us.' Holly looked at her mum, who was looking anxiously at Poppy.

'Sure.' Poppy shrugged. 'Anything for my lovely sister.' Laura smiled and patted her oldest daughter gently on the shoulder, vacantly pretending not to notice that the teenager had flinched at being touched.

Poppy handed Holly a beautifully wrapped present. Tearing off the paper in a hurry didn't seem right, so Holly opened it carefully, taking her time. Inside was a small jewellery box containing a pair of beautiful stud earrings. 'Wow, thank you, Poppy. But I don't have my ears pierced...'

'Duh, I know that, I will meet you after school, we have an appointment at The Salon...' Before Poppy could even finish her sentence, Holly leapt out of bed and cuddled her sister. 'Love you, love you, love you!'

As she opened the gift from her mother and discovered a brand new, awesome, latest edition iPhone, Holly screeched and hugged her mum tightly. Being ten was fantastic so far and it was only ten past six in the morning! She couldn't wait to get to school now and tell Louise and Otterlie about her presents.

Chapter 2

They pulled up in the silver Range Rover into the familiar lay-by outside Mimosa Primary School. There were pupils, parents and teachers milling about and excited babbles of children happy to see each other after the summer break. The new reception-aged children stood clinging to the teary adults with them. They looked so tiny standing there swamped in their oversized uniforms. Holly leaned over to her mum and gave her a big hug.

'Love you, Mum, have a good day at work. See you later, Poppy, good luck at your first day at college... Oh, there's Otterlie... See ya at three o'clock, Pops, bye...'

Holly gathered up all her bags, pausing to stroke the red fluff back into place, jumped out of the car, slammed the door and went rushing after her friend. Laura turned to her oldest daughter and smiled at her.

'She's so happy to go back to school. Do you remember those days?'

Poppy just shrugged and humphed in response to her mum's question.

'Right, let's get you to your first day too. New chapter of your life starting today, Pops. You might make some new friends...'

As they drove slowly back onto the main road and headed towards the large college in the city, Poppy glanced suspiciously at her mother to determine if the remark had been meant sarcastically. Deciding it wasn't, she smiled and shrugged. 'I have friends though,' she replied. Almost under her breath she murmured, 'Sometimes they are a bit much.'

Holly ran towards Otterlie. It was actually pretty good to be coming back to Mimosa. She had missed the normality of the routine and structure of being at school, although she would never admit that to her friends!

'Happy birthday to you,' sang Otterlie as she pulled her friend into a bear hug. 'Missed you. The Aimee-mum did this to my jumper, I can't suck it or stick my thumb through any more. Look!' She held out her sleeve to show Holly the tight, neat stitches her newly appointed stepmum had performed on the cuff. 'She said to me that, even if we can't afford a new one, I don't have to look like a tramp.'

They walked with their arms linked, chattering animatedly through the front playground. Holly suddenly let out a laughing scream as the other member of their best friend trio jumped onto her back.

'All right, Hols and Ottie, did you miss me? Look at my tan, the agency nearly had a fit as they were worried my sunburn might ruin the forest shoot, oh yeah, it's your birthday, don't worry, Hols – my mum is bringing your present after school, she said it might not be ideal to have it in the class on the first day, oh my, look at Luke's hair – it's got a green tinge! Bertie had best not get any ideas, Mum will throw a fit!' Louise paused her nonstop monologue greeting as they looked past the gaggles of children on the playground towards their new class teacher, Mrs Redleigh, who was walking down the steps at the front of the Victorian building. Mr George suddenly appeared behind her and, bounding past like a gazelle, he then headed towards a group of boys who were in the same class as the three best friends.

'Uh oh,' said Holly, 'he's heading towards green-haired Luke and your brother too, Louise.'

Together, the girls stood still with their arms linked and watched Mr George as he hi-fived the boys in the group. Even

Louise's twin, Bertie, joined in, holding his hand up the same as his peers. Louise breathed a sigh of relief. She was glad they had Mr George as their Teaching Assistant this year.

Bertie often found new situations very difficult and she couldn't face one of his meltdowns this early in the morning. The smile died on Holly's face though as she turned back around and was just in time to see a group of sniggering girls pulling faces, pointing in her direction and snorting like hippos. She felt the tears prickle in her eyes. Maybe it wasn't so great to be back at school. Otterlie nudged her and whispered in her ear, 'Ugly idiots, don't worry, they've been busted…'

'Isla, Esther, Polly come here,' ordered Mrs Redleigh in her officious teacher voice. 'You girls are in Summer Class now and, as you will very shortly find out, we have rules and expectations. Pulling faces and being mean is definitely unacceptable. You three will be on my watch list for the day, so I fully expect you to redeem yourselves!' The offending girls were remorseful enough to look sheepish and they visibly squirmed uncomfortably under their new teacher's glare.

Mrs Redleigh seemed to wink at Holly, although Holly wasn't sure if it was a trick of the light because just then the teacher looked around and blew her whistle shrilly. The playground noise ceased immediately. All the pupils stood silently waiting for the second whistle, so they could line up with their new class teachers, ready to go into the building. The parents who were standing with the tiny, new reception-aged children looked panicked and glanced round anxiously at each other, clearly unsure of the correct protocol. Holly watched the headteacher, Mrs Rose, walk briskly towards them and help shepherd away the floundering adults so the Reception Class staff could get the little ones in and settled.

She remembered her first day at Mimosa Primary all those years ago and thought back to how welcoming and relaxed it had been, once they had been taken in and sat down on the carpet. Her mum had been newly widowed, meaning that Holly hadn't had the correct school shoes or a reading bookbag but the teachers had fussed around and made her feel extra special and well looked after. She knew the teachers and TAs would soon settle down the new cohort.

The whistle blew again and Mrs Redleigh stood in the Year Five section of the playground with her arms outstretched in front of her. 'Summer Class right here,' she called. 'Mr George, please can you bring up the end of our line?'

'Aye aye, Captain,' saluted Mr George as he skipped towards the back of the line, gathering up Bertie and Arasuli on his way. They had been hovering by the Year Four section looking unsure and worried.

The two boys could be seen to visibly relax as the lovable, vibrantly coloured but smartly dressed TA showed them to their spaces in the Summer Class line.

'Thirty fresh new faces for us, Mrs R, ready when you are.'

Mrs Redleigh rolled her eyes in good humour at Mr George. Smiling affectionately at her new class, she turned and led them into the old, brick building. The school had been expanded over the previous decade, with several new classrooms added by an adjoining link corridor which also opened into the large school hall. The original main entrance, through which they all now trooped under the bell tower archway, had welcomed many generations of children over the years, some of them the parents and grandparents of the current Summer Class.

Chapter 3

Holly and her eager classmates found their newly named pegs, which were situated outside their new classroom in the older part of the building. After opening her rucksack and removing her water bottle and new pencil case, which contained her recently purchased stationery, she followed her friends into the bright, airy room.

Mrs Redleigh had the whole class stand around the outside of the tables in a large semi-circle whilst she went through the register, allocating each child a pre-determined seat as she called their name.

Holly was placed near the back of the room on a table of six along with Bertie, Ruby, Luna, Leo and much to her disgust, Isla, one of the girls who seemed to think it was okay to make fun of others. Holly thought the horsey-looking, blonde-haired girl was spiteful and she felt disgruntled that she had been expected to share a table with someone who was so unpleasant. Glancing around the room, it seemed that Mrs Redleigh had deliberately separated all friendship groups and strategically placed the children where nobody would have any fun. She caught Louise's eyeroll and made a face back at her friend who seemed to be groaning internally.

'Poor Lou,' thought Holly. Her friend had been put on a front table with Arasuli. He was nice enough but hardly said anything as his English wasn't very strong yet. He had only joined them in

Spring Class a few weeks before the end of the previous term. They all knew he had had a tough time and was a Syrian refugee but until he became more confident in his ability to join in and communicate, Holly knew he would struggle to feel like part of the class.

Maybe Mrs Redleigh had a method to her madness after all. Louise constantly chattered nonstop so if anyone could teach him new language skills, it would be her!

Otterlie was on the table behind Bertie's chair so Holly quickly positioned her own seat, so it was angled with the best view of her friend.

Mr George nudged her conspiringly as he walked past her seat. He was handing out paper and sharpened pencils in brightly decorated pots, one for each table group.

'Happy birthday, Miss Holly Rivers. Don't worry, I know Mrs R hasn't forgotten, I saw the cake with my own eyes this morning. Just hope the other staff don't get there first!' He grinned at her then carried on weaving in and out of the tables, humming the Happy Birthday song quietly.

Mrs Redleigh instructed the class to use the mirrors that she had asked Luna to hand out. Summer Class was then tasked with the challenge of studying their own face and sketching a self-portrait.

'Concentrate, boys and girls. These will be displayed on the wall all year!' informed Mr George as he floated around the room offering encouragement.

The first day of being in Year Five passed in a whirlwind of learning new class routines, an assembly which included a serenade of Happy Birthday for Holly and the five other children who had celebrated their respective birthdays throughout the summer holidays. Mr George had amazingly performed an onstage harmony! Break and lunch time playground politics continued and the seemingly unfair Mrs Redleigh had even forced them to do a Reading and Maths test.

The highlight of the day though was being given the privilege of using a sharp, serrated knife to cut the incredible cake creation that Mrs Redleigh had made, into thirty-two equal-sized slices. Holly had panicked when told she was going to be the one teaching her classmates about fractions but cutting the cake and handing out the slices hadn't seemed too much like a Maths lesson.

As promised, Poppy was waiting with her mum for Holly at the school entrance. The family drove into the city to the popular, trendy salon and Poppy held her sister's hand as the purple-haired body piercer put a pretty, diamond stud through each of Holly's ears. It stung a bit, only for a few minutes but Holly made no noise as she wanted Poppy to be proud of her! Whilst Poppy was paying, after proudly showing that she was old enough to have responsibility for her sister by producing her passport, Holly clutched the aftercare solution she had been given and wandered over to the brightly decorated area of the shop, where her mum was chatting animatedly to the slightly scary looking tattoo artist. They seemed to know each other. As Laura saw her daughter approaching, she subtly pocketed the small bag she had just been given and held out her arms to her daughter. 'Aw, Holiboos, you look so grown up. Poppy was right to convince me to let her treat you to this.'

Hearing her name, Poppy joined them at the front of the salon. 'What do you say about letting Holly convince you to let me have my nose pierced then?' Poppy grinned at her mother and rolled her eyes as Laura glanced worriedly at the display of piercing pictures and photographs behind them. 'Only joking,

Mum, I'll wait for Christmas. Today is about Holly!'

The three of them went home via a quick trip to McDonalds. As they approached their driveway, Holly squealed with excitement because she could see Louise's mum's car waiting on the gravel. Laura parked next to them and got out smiling, hurrying up to the twins' mum, Claudette. The two adults began whispering and gesticulating towards the back of the Bentley Bentayga where Bertie sat with his noise-cancelling headphones on, holding a large box. Holly and Poppy ran over to stand with Louise who, after admiring her friend's new sparkling earrings, proceeded to block their sight of the car by jumping and skipping around being generally irritating as far as the others were concerned.

Just when the girls thought they couldn't take the suspense anymore and Louise was about to get pushed aside in the excitement, Claudette opened the back door of the car and took the box from Bertie who mumbled to his mother that he was happy to stay in the car with his iPad. Shrieking girls and excitement made him uncomfortable.

The rest of them all went into the house, following Laura who led them to the lounge, kicking aside a couple of stray shoes on the way. Louise pushed the door shut behind her and they all sat around the box which Claudette had placed on the coffee table.

'So… happy birthday, Holly,' began Claudette, 'I was backset on the twins' latest modelling shoot and I heard the photographer say he might need some help with finding homes for these cuties. I immediately thought of your family. Obviously I had to check with your mum, but she agreed with me that it was a good idea…' She trailed off as her daughter eagerly opened the box and gently took out a squirming ball of fluff and handed it to her best friend. Holly's heart instantly melted as she stroked the young, tabby kitten who was purring rhythmically in her arms.

Laura looked towards her oldest daughter who was sitting on the floor with her back resting against the sofa, looking like her thoughts were a million miles away. 'There's one for you too, Poppy.' She said it quietly as she assessed the reaction her comment would receive. She needn't have worried as Poppy reached forward and took the proffered kitten from Claudette with tears of gratitude bright in her eyes.

Chapter 4

The next few weeks passed by in a whirl of back-to-school routine for Holly and her family. The new additions had become firmly established members of the household. Poppy had named her kitten Shady. Holly, after much deliberation, called hers Rufus. The little fluffballs had truly made themselves at home and had complete freedom to roam the house. Laura had abandoned her original idea of them not being allowed in the girls' bedrooms as even Poppy had seemed to mellow in her attitude towards her mother when she had Shady to cuddle up with at night time.

Holly was still regularly worried about her sister. The anxiety she felt every time Poppy disappeared into the red car, which was often lurking at the end of their drive, turned somersaults of deep unease in her stomach. These friends of Poppy's did not seem to make her sister very happy.

She wasn't sure how much her mum despaired any more though because in the last few days, Laura had begun to retreat back into the distant, shaky, ghost of a mother who forgot to go shopping and sometimes even forgot to get dressed for the school run.

The gang of mean girls in Summer Class noticed Laura's unkempt look the next morning and Holly felt close to tears as she stood waiting on the playground for Louise to join her and Otterlie. Otterlie tried to be understanding but she was slightly preoccupied with having to deal with a new stepmother and stepbrother living in her house. Her home life had suddenly been turned upside down.

Holly tried her hardest to tune back into Otterlie's description of how awful her new stepbrother was. Something about him deliberately kicking her every time she walked past his room. He consistently moaned about this to his mum because, as he was older than Otterlie, he felt he should have had her bigger bedroom when he and his mum had moved in. It seemed that Aimee-mum agreed with Otterlie's dad that it was tough luck and he had to be grateful he had a room at all. Of course, as Otterlie was discovering, and she had the bruises to prove it, this just made him hold more of a grudge against her. Holly murmured sympathetically. She really did feel sorry for her friend, but she was also very aware of the looks and stage-whispering coming from the gossiping, gesturing children who were huddled near the playground benches.

Louise and Bertie burst through the school gate just as Mrs Redleigh blew the morning whistle for the children to line up in their class area of the playground. As Holly got into her place in the Summer Class order, Isla and Polly bumped and jostled her deliberately, almost knocking her over. As she stumbled and tried to get sympathetic attention from Louise or Otterlie, Polly leaned forward and whispered spitefully in Holly's ear, 'Your mum is a mess again. My dad says she should go to rehab and sort herself out. You'll end up in care because your dad is dead, your sister is a tramp and you're practically an orphan!'

Holly felt the tears well up in her eyes. As she followed her class line into school, she could hardly catch her breath because of the effort it was taking not to cry and give Polly the satisfaction of knowing she'd got to her.

Just before they went into the classroom, Mr George caught

Mrs Redleigh's eye who nodded back her agreement at him. He then gently touched Holly's arm and guided her towards the empty school library. He sat her down on the large, brightly coloured bean bags, then shimmied and danced towards the big box of tissues the librarian kept on her desk. Giving the kindly, old and slightly deaf lady a wink and a bow, he then pulled up another equally brightly coloured beanbag and flopped down on it dramatically while handing Holly the tissues. 'We've got an exciting assembly planned today, Holly. Isla and Luna's dads are coming in to talk about their jobs as firefighters. You can have a front row seat if you agree to come and help me set up the chairs in the hall.' Holly managed a watery smile in response and nodded at her TA. 'Anything you want to talk about?' Mr George asked gently.

Holly thought about all the worries that were swirling around in her head; dealing with the nasty, relentless comments from some of her peers, her mum forgetting to look after herself or to act like a normal mum, Poppy staying out more and more and often seeming extremely sad when she was home, worrying she had forgotten what her dad's face looked like- as she had been only four when he died. She thought her feelings would burst out of her like a cascading waterfall and she mournfully wished she was at home, cuddling up with Rufus. Suddenly, the thought of her kitten's cute little face and looking forward to him greeting her when she got home each day, seemed to melt her worries into the background and they didn't seem quite so overwhelming. She blew her nose on the tissue and looked up enquiringly at Mr George's face. 'What's rehab?'

Mr George stood up and grabbed her hands to pull her to her feet. He could tell that Holly was more composed but was still teetering on feeling fragile and he was aware of the troubled look which still lurked in her eyes. He would speak to Mrs Redleigh later about Holly joining the waiting list to see the much-in-demand school counsellor, Miss Buzzing. As far as he knew, only Arasuli was currently on the list in front of her.

As they sauntered towards the hall, he thought about how to answer her question without knowing the full reason it had been on Holly's mind. He knew better than to force her to talk or to ask any leading questions. He smiled at her and pointed towards the stack of chairs that needed setting out into rows. 'Rehab is a special place where people go to get better from an illness or addiction. They are looked after and helped by professional, caring staff.'

'Oh,' said Holly, as she lined up the chairs. 'So, it's not a bad place to go where you make your children orphans?'

Mr George didn't really know how to answer that. He felt himself in the rare situation of being stuck for something to say. The conversation made him feel uneasy because, as a child, he had watched as his own father struggled to battle crippling gambling demons. 'Rehab can be a very positive step, Holly, but sometimes some people have to realise they need to be there for themselves as well as their families.' He pulled down the screen for the projector and turned on the speakers by the stage. Pharrell Williams' song "Happy" blasted out into the room and Holly went to take her place in the line of Summer Class children filing into the hall. She felt a lot calmer now and was glad that she hadn't had to go into the class for the normal morning activities.

Mrs Redleigh led the children in their usual fun-filled Wednesday singing assembly, which included the enthusiastic and willing teachers and teaching assistants singing solos. Mr George even backflipped across the stage, which caused all the children to cheer and whoop with excitement, but they settled back down quickly when he got told off for not adhering to the health and safety rules. Once they had finished learning a new song about celebrating Harvest Festival, the lower school year groups filed back to their classrooms just leaving Years Five and Six sitting in the hall. Mrs Redleigh handed over the iPad to the group of four firefighters who looked like they had thoroughly enjoyed the assembly experience.

The large screen came to life with images of different scenarios including a beach scene and storm damage, showing various people being rescued by firefighters. They presented it exceptionally well, inviting children to come to the front to role play and try on a selection of uniform and try out equipment. From her position in the front row, Holly unexpectedly saw movement out of the corner of her eye.

Turning her head, she could see that Arasuli was rocking frantically backwards and forwards with his arms wrapped tightly around his body, tears streaming down his face. Before Holly could get the attention of Mrs Redleigh, to alert her to the boy's distress, he let out a guttural, animal-like howl and then began whimpering uncontrollably. Mrs Redleigh rushed to his side and scooped him up in her arms, enveloping him in a bear hug. As his whimpering quietened and she led him out of the hall towards Miss Buzzing's quiet den area, the children around the hall lost the ability to focus on the firefighters, who were still gallantly trying to distract and engage the audience, and the noise level rose. Bertie suddenly screamed and held his hands over his ears, the decibel volume had become too much for him and he lost control. He jumped up and down, flapping his hands, repeatedly shouting, 'Shut up, shut up, shut up.' Some of the children, who were used to Bertie's outbursts, sniggered. Others managed to look remorseful and moved their chairs away to give him some space. Louise glared at the boys who were winding her brother up and rose out of her seat until Otterlie grabbed her into a hug and kept her calm. Bertie had gone beyond the "reasoning with his sister" stage and wasn't even aware she was there. He picked up the chair nearest to him and began banging it repetitively on the wall.

Mrs Redleigh came back into the hall to witness Mr George calmly and efficiently lining up the two classes to remove them from the situation. The Year Six teacher and his TA weren't there as they had used the opportunity of an extended assembly to fit in some planning time. The poor firefighters looked flustered and unsure what to do. They were standing chatting nervously on the front of the stage. Mrs Redleigh took charge of the issues at hand and whilst placing some soft cushions around Bertie, she swiftly moved the rest of the chairs out of harm's way and thanked the visitors profusely for a great assembly. She sent them off to the staffroom for a cup of tea and assured them someone would be in to help them pack up their equipment as soon as possible. 'Thank you so much, Mr George. Please could you take the children out for an early break while I stay with Bertie?' She smiled at him and he responded with a half-smile, a salute and mimed the action of hanging himself with his tie. 'What a morning!' she said, almost to herself, as she took a deep breath and turned to comfort Bertie who was now lying on the floor, spent and exhausted.

Because Mr George had been in the library first thing with Holly, both he and Mrs Redleigh had forgotten to give Bertie his ear defenders before going into assembly.

Chapter 5

Arasuli returned to the classroom after lunch, having spent an extremely emotional morning having emergency therapy. Bertie surprised everyone by running up, hugging him and inviting him to have dinner at his house. This was a social progression milestone for each boy and both the adults in the room felt overwhelmed and a little teary with the pride they experienced. Holly caught Louise's eye and they shared a smile. Holly knew how much her friend worried about her twin.

That evening, Louise phoned Holly on her new mobile and invited her for a sleepover on Friday after school. Otterlie was going to be there too and Bertie had invited Arasuli as promised. Louise chattered away on the phone for nearly an hour, describing and planning what they would get up to and repeating the conversation she had overheard between her parents who had worried how both the boys would cope. 'It's okay though, we will help them. Arasuli talks to me sometimes in class, I know his English is getting better!'

After the call, Holly ran downstairs to check Claudette had messaged her mum, to confirm the sleepover.

She discovered Laura frantically scrubbing the rustic kitchen table, music pounding from the earphones secured tightly in each ear. There was a manic look on her face and her eyes were bright. Holly tried smiling at her mum, then cuddled her to try and get some attention. Laura stopped scrubbing and looked at her daughter. 'The stain is still there, Holly, it won't ever go away!'

Holly knew the story of the stain and the reason they still kept the large antique table, even though it took up so much room in the kitchen. Her dad's grandfather had crafted the table himself from an oak tree which had been damaged by a German pilot during World War Two. The table had lots of history and had been passed down in the Wills of all the oldest children on her dad's side of the family. She knew it would belong to Poppy one day, when her sister eventually had a house of her own. The stain though, had been caused by her dad on the morning that he left the house and never returned.

Poppy had been ten and Holly four that fateful, early summer's day. They had been playing in the garden with the hose, splashing each other and filling up the paddling pool while their parents enjoyed a lazy, cooked, adult-only breakfast in the kitchen. The hose had suddenly pinged off from the kitchen tap and water had sprayed all over the room, causing their dad, Marcus, to jump up to protect his wife from the torrent. He had slipped in the puddle on the floor tiles and knocked a bottle of red wine off the worktop which had smashed all over the table. Hence the stain. Once the shrieking laughter and pandemonium had been calmed and the kitchen restored to its usual dry, tidy state, Marcus had kissed his family goodbye and then gone out to the supermarket to buy some stain-remover for the table. He had been killed instantly in a head-on collision with an articulated lorry, whose driver had been scrolling through Facebook whilst driving. Although she had only been young, Holly knew that, from then on, the regular laughter in her house had faded away to be replaced with overwhelming sadness because her dad had failed to come home. Six years later, it still weighed down upon her family like low, heavy storm clouds.

Giving her mum an extra tight cuddle and enjoying the sensation of her mum absently stroking her hair, Holly tentatively asked what was for dinner. She had looked in the fridge when she had first arrived home from school and had not seen much except for the cat food she had put down for Rufus and Shady. Part of her was worried about staying out at Louise's house on Friday. If Poppy was out too, which was highly probable, then she knew her mum wouldn't remember to eat, even though she would have ordered a food shop to be delivered by then. Laura sighed in response and phoned for takeaway. Again.

Friday afternoon seemed to drag by so slowly for the majority of Summer Class. Mr George announced mock-conspiringly to Mrs Redleigh that he could smell the weekend coming! There seemed to be a general feeling of excitement rippling amongst the children and even the usual snide comments from Isla, Esther and Polly could not ruin Holly's happy mood. Bertie was on cloud nine. He kept walking up to Arasuli, jumping up and down, then circling the classroom before returning to his seat where he would fidget for a while and then get up again.

Mrs Redleigh threw her hands in the air. 'Right, books away, tables tidied. First table ready will be the first group I send to line up by the door for special, extra breaktime!' The mood lifted even more as the class cheered and scrambled to organise and tidy their work area.

Mr George grabbed his sunglasses and hi-fived the children as they trooped out to the playground.

'Good call, Mrs R,' he exclaimed.

'What a week!' she replied with a grin.

Going to Louise and Bertie's house was always an experience. Once through the front door you had to proceed through a long, plant-filled hallway. The ceiling-brushing, large-leafed organic varieties in enormous, ornate pots that lined the corridor, always made Holly feel that she was a princess walking past her waving and bowing subjects. As she whispered this thought to Otterlie, who nodded in agreement, they almost bumped into the back of Arasuli who had stopped dead in front of them and was just looking around with wide-eyed awe.

Bertie, jumping up and down with the overwhelming anticipation of having his friend to his house, beckoned for Arasuli to follow him. The boys raced off up the creaky, but carpeted, stairs to his space-themed bedroom. As the girls went through the kitchen to see what snacks Claudette was finding, they could hear Bertie talking excitedly to Arasuli and loud thumps which sounded like the ceiling would suddenly produce a boy's leg or two through a crack in the plaster. Claudette visibly winced but did not comment on the noise from above as she pushed bowls full of fruit salad towards Louise and her friends. 'Why don't you girls go outside? You might get more peace in the treehouse!'

Louise's dad, Stephen, popped out to say hello to the girls when he arrived home from his job in the city. He had come home early, specially to witness his son having a friend over for dinner. It was such a momentous occasion, he wanted to be part of it. Holly couldn't remember what his job was, but she knew that Louise often missed him as he was away a lot, travelling around the world, having important meetings. 'Hi, darling,' he called up the wooden ladder. 'Hi, Otterlie. Hi, Holly.' The girls scrambled back into the beautifully crafted treehouse as Stephen's head and shoulders appeared through the trap door. 'Looks lovely and cosy in here, girls, Mum says pizza in five minutes.'

'Pizza!' exclaimed Louise is disbelief. 'Mum won't let us

have pizza, even if me and Bertie do have friends round! She is taking us to a new shoot at the weekend, isn't she?' Holly and Otterlie looked at each other questionably. They knew that dinner at their friend's house was always super healthy and delicious, lovingly prepared from scratch by Claudette. Both Louise and Bertie were signed up to an exclusive modelling agency and regularly represented well-known brands by promoting their products. Louise had also recently been in an advertising campaign, encouraging viewers to donate to the sadly, much-needed, new local foodbank. Her haunting, ethereal looks had been captured on camera portraying a deprived, malnourished child. Louise's own circumstances were the complete opposite and the fortunate twins were never without any luxury. Stephen and Claudette had been so moved by the cause that they had sent a large cheque to kickstart the fundraising and Claudette had applied to be a volunteer at the village hall, sorting out the donated food into parcels for families in need.

Stephen smiled and winked at his daughter. 'Well, it's not a calorie laden, greasy, artery clogging, takeaway pizza... Your mum has made pitta bread pizzas, using fresh ingredients. She's put out so many choices of toppings I'm sure we'll be at the table all evening creating our dinner!'

As he disappeared back through the hole in the wooden floor, the girls whooped and hid away the secret mission ideas notebook they had been working on. None of them wanted Bertie to find it as one of their plans involved stopping Luke, Aidens and a few other boys in their class from reacting negatively whenever Bertie had one of his episodes. The girls knew that this caused him extra stress and it took him longer to be able to calm down again.

They scrambled down from the treehouse and skipped

towards the dining room; all five children were in high spirits as they settled around the flamboyantly presented feast laid out on the table.

Arasuli was quiet but polite as he helped himself to a variety of toppings for his pizza. Claudette thought he was probably overwhelmed by the chatter from the girls, so she didn't pressurise him by asking too many questions about his home life. They all knew he'd had a tough time and was now living in a new, strange country without his parents or full knowledge of the language but, reassuringly, he seemed as content as any other nine/ten-year-old as he and Bertie deliberately nudged each other and grinned as they reached for the food.

Because of Bertie's limited social experiences, it had been agreed that although Holly and Otterlie would be sleeping over, Arasuli would be driven home after dinner on this first occasion. Assured that he was welcome back any time, this arrangement suited Arasuli, who was starting to feel a bit apprehensive. After the meal had finished, Bertie began to seem agitated about his evening routine being disrupted. Not wanting their guest to feel uncomfortable, Stephen asked the three girls to accompany him on the ride to drop Arasuli home, whilst Claudette stayed to reassure Bertie that his play date had gone well and get him back into the comfortable zone of his familiar daily schedule.

Somehow, Holly ended up in the front seat. Louise, Otterlie and Arasuli bundled into the back of the stately SUV. Holly didn't mind. She liked her friend's dad and he chattered to her, asking about her mum, sister and the kittens. She didn't really know what to say to describe her mum's current low state, her distant sister, or the never-ending battle of refilling the empty fridge so, avoiding those questions, she mumbled that they were fine. She then became much more animated, describing the recent antics of the much-loved kittens.

Twenty-year-old Amir Deeb appeared from a wooden side gate as they pulled up outside a row of shops with shabby, run-down maisonettes above them. He had been working hard all day, long hours of manual labour on a local farm, and had not been home long but he had found himself missing his nephew, Arasuli, much more than he thought possible. He was very happy that the boy had made friends finally, almost six months after the traumatically dangerous and life-changing journey they had taken together to enter the United Kingdom.

Parking on the kerb, Stephen got out, held open the back door for Arasuli and then introduced himself to Arasuli's uncle and legal guardian. While the two men made small talk, with Amir patting Arasuli's head protectively, Holly happened to look up and she gasped, causing the girls in the backseat to follow her gaze.

The notoriously familiar red car had pulled up onto the brightly lit pavement in front of them. Holly witnessed her sleepy, stumbling sister being pulled roughly from the front seat and half dragged, half carried towards a door adjoining the boarded-up kebab shop entrance, which was only a few doors down from where Arasuli lived.

Chapter 6

Naïve and innocent enough to not realise the potential implications of the situation, Holly sprang out of the car and rushed towards the men who were bundling her pitiful sister into a dark, damp hallway, which led to a stale smelling staircase. Her two friends were right behind her. They didn't get very far because, before they could enter the dingy building, the door was firmly slammed in their faces. Stephen, Amir and Arasuli came running up to assess what on earth was going on and Holly burst into tears of panic and frustration. 'Poppy is in there. She doesn't look very well, the other people looked scary and evil. Please help her.' Holly was sobbing so hard that her words were hard to decipher but Stephen understood the general gist. Hopefully, there was a reasonable explanation and no harm was being done but he had a bad feeling stirring in his gut. He looked at Amir, he was young; only just an adult, but his eyes told a story of survival and strength. He was physically fit too, long hours of heavy lifting each day matched with Stephen's dedication to the gym.

Amir nodded at Stephen. He understood the predicament. 'You four need to get into the car and lock the doors,' ordered Stephen. 'Do not move from the car until we are back. If we are not here in ten minutes, call the police. You've got your phone, haven't you, Holly?' As she nodded through her sobs, Louise took charge and pushed her friends towards the car. All four children huddled in the back seat and watched as the two men knocked hard. They then took a step back whilst waiting to see what would greet them behind the door.

Almost immediately, the door was violently yanked open and three men glared out at the interruption to their evening. The children, locked safely in the car, couldn't fully hear what was being said, especially not over Holly's snotty sobs and gasps as she tried to catch her breath, but they were aware of the aggressive gesturing and raised voices. Lights had appeared in a few other windows along the street and curtains were twitching as curious neighbours tried to see what was occurring. Suddenly, a fourth man, about Amir's age, appeared behind the others in the doorway and he shoved a dishevelled, dazed Poppy towards Stephen, before disappearing back into the gloom.

Holly yelped with relief at seeing her sister. The men, obviously realising their actions might have unwanted consequences, seemed to now be threatening Amir and pointing menacingly towards the cowering occupants of the car. Beads of sweat were visible on their dark-bearded, middle-aged faces as they hurried back inside.

Turning away from the shabby property and leading Poppy to safety, Stephen took a deep breath. He'd been very worried about how that could have played out very differently and was well aware it could have been far worse than it already was if the younger man hadn't made the abrupt choice to return Poppy to him. He also now felt a sense of responsibility for his comrade as the intimidating, undesirable men had seemed to recognise Amir and obviously knew he lived nearby, with young Arasuli.

Jumbled thoughts of what the next course of action should be tumbled round in Stephen's head as he propelled the intoxicated teenager forward. He knew all eight of them wouldn't fit in his Bentley. He was also aware, not only did the police need to be called, as well as Laura, to meet them at the hospital, he knew too that it was too dangerous to leave Arasuli and Amir alone in the vicinity of the unpredictable thugs.

Help to his dilemma arrived in the form of a large Indian family who had witnessed some of what had happened from their maisonette windows. Stephen sat a shell-shocked Poppy in the front seat of his waiting vehicle while he spoke quickly and quietly with several of the adults, who had come out to offer their support. They all agreed that the top priority was to get Poppy checked over while also keeping the small, refugee Deeb family safe. Stephen promised them he would contact the police. Hearing the word police, Amir launched into an outburst of Syrian and began shaking his head and trembling. Arasuli, seeing his uncle's distressed state, tentatively untangled himself from the crying girls and went to stand by the adults. 'Please, please, no Police,' translated Arasuli in his newly learned grasp of the English language. 'They won't let us stay together. I'll be separated from my uncle and it will be bad, please!' Understanding that this was an overly complex issue and knowing what Amir could have risked by supporting his attempt to reason with the men holding Poppy, Stephen promised he would do everything in his power to help them.

Aware that Stephen had to get Poppy to hospital and away from this street, the kind-hearted Indians led the vulnerable Syrians into their home until somewhere safer could be found for them. Figuring that it was better to leave the area instead of hanging around for an ambulance and risking the men coming back out, Stephen decided to drive straight to the city himself.

The car journey was a blur for Holly. She wasn't really sure what had happened to her sister, but she knew Poppy was ill and in pain. The sixteen-year-old was slumped in the passenger seat and her head kept lolling forward whenever grim-faced Stephen turned a corner or braked. Otterlie and Louise sat on either side of Holly and although all three girls were tightly holding hands none of them spoke. As they neared the large A and E facility in the city, Stephen caught Holly's eye in the rear-view mirror. 'Call your mum again, Holly. If there's still no answer, text and tell her to get to the hospital ASAP.' Holly had been trying to get through on and off for the whole tense twenty-minute journey, but she kept being diverted to voicemail. She wished she had remembered to save her house phone number into her contacts as her mum had asked her to when she first got the phone for her birthday.

Claudette and Bertie arrived at the hospital to sit in the waiting room with the girls. The police had requested that they wait a while so statements could be taken. Stephen was still by Poppy's side as nobody could get hold of Laura.

Holly had been briefly allowed in to see her sister who was hooked up to various machines with a tube connected to the back of her hand. Poppy had fluttered her eyelashes sleepily but had managed a watery smile, 'You saved me, Hols. Thank you.' Reassured by the nurses that Poppy was okay, Holly let herself be led back out to the others. Otterlie hugged her friend and then stood up and waved as her dad came through the automatic doors with Holly's mum. He had been to the house to collect Laura and had finally managed to rouse her from the alcohol and narcotic induced coma. Luckily, the conservatory door had been left ajar so he'd been able to get in. After a brisk, cold shower and a strong coffee, Laura had been mortified and wracked with guilt after learning her eldest daughter was in a hospital bed. On the fraught ride to A and E, Jonny Oapie, Otterlie's dad, had reassuringly promised to never breathe a word about how he had found her to anyone, not even to his new wife, Aimee.

Laura would be staying by Poppy's bedside, Stephen and the police were going to find somewhere safe for Amir and Arasuli. Bertie was clearly uncomfortable at the disruption to his routine, so Claudette arranged with Jonny that Holly would go back and stay with him and Otterlie.

Holly felt overwhelmed with emotional exhaustion, especially after receiving hugs from so many people. Although she was unsure about leaving her mum and sister, she was glad that she would be staying with Otterlie. They were to follow Claudette and the twins home first to collect her overnight bag. It had been an exceptionally long day!

Chapter 7

The next day, Holly and Otterlie slept in until mid-morning. Aimee's teenage son had gone to his dad's house for the weekend, so the girls were the only children in the house. Jonny was determined to keep the girls busy so there was no time for Holly to dwell on last night's events.

After a delicious cooked brunch, he sent Otterlie upstairs to find swimming costumes, towels and goggles for all of them. He looked at Holly, 'I've spoken to your mum. Poppy is going to be okay. She's probably going to be in hospital for one more night as she has a small fracture in her clavicle.' He gestured to his collarbone to answer the question in Holly's eyes. 'There will be an investigation and the police might need to speak to you girls and Arasuli again about what you saw but, because you all did so well last night at the hospital, they will probably wait until Monday and pop in and see you at school.' Jonny kept his tone light; he didn't want to distress Holly but nor did he want her worrying about not knowing what was going on.

They drove to the leisure centre and had a great time in the pool. Holly could see why Otterlie liked her new stepmother. Aimee was great fun. She scrambled across the large inflatable obstacle course with them, shrieking with laughter and mock horror every time she fell off with a splash. Jonny stood at the side of the smaller, extra-deep pool and cheered on all three of them as they climbed up the steps to the highest diving board. Otterlie said that it was because he had a bad back that he couldn't join them. Neither of the girls had been brave enough to venture over to this part of the pool before. Aimee went first, executing a perfectly graceful backwards dive. She had been in training for the Olympic swimming team when she was younger, but had given it up when she had broken her leg while being pregnant with her son.

Otterlie and Holly looked nervously at the water from their position at the top of the steps. It seemed a long way down. They had a quick game of Rock, Paper, Scissors to see who would go first and Holly won, so Otterlie had to go first. She watched her friend take a deep breath and step onto the wobbly board. Otterlie closed her eyes as she jumped off and when she emerged, laughing to swim towards Aimee's waiting arms, Holly knew that it was now her turn. She wasn't sure if it was the board or her legs that were shaking so hard as she edged forward and peered down to where the others were waiting. The butterflies were doing a frenzied dance in her stomach and a big part of her wanted to turn around, but walking back along the thin plastic didn't seem any less terrifying. 'Come on, Hols, you can do it!' Otterlie's encouraging voice floated upwards.

'I'll be right here, Holly. You'll be fine,' Aimee reassured her. Holly stepped forward into nothingness and gasped when the water cushioned her. Kicking for the surface she smilingly, with a huge sense of achievement, swam towards the cheers and whoops from her friend and her family.

Once they were changed and Aimee had spent what had seemed like hours helping Otterlie get her gorgeous, but often unruly afro back under control, Jonny declared that he was starving so he treated them all to a McDonald's before they went home.

After spending another night at her friend's house, Jonny and

Otterlie drove Holly home the next morning. Laura greeted them at the door and invited them in. Although she looked tired, the vacant, disinterested haze had gone from her eyes and Holly could tell the proper mumsy mum was back. As she put the kettle on, her eyes met Jonny's. 'Thank you so much,' she spoke quietly. 'If there is any good to come out of this, I've had a sharp wake up shock. My poor, poor baby.'

Jonny hugged her tight. 'We are all here for you, Laura. I made that promise to you when Marcus died, and I stand by it forever.' He and Marcus had been friends long before any of their children had been born. He glanced at the girls and seeing they were fully engaged with pampering the kittens he continued, 'Any updates?'

Holly pricked up her ears but pretended to be absorbed with Rufus and Shady. She couldn't hear everything the adults were whispering about, but the odd words like ring, trafficking, court case carried across the kitchen. Maybe they weren't talking about Poppy after all. It seemed to be more like one of the usual, boring adult conversations, advocating for the local State Of The Road campaign in the village.

After Otterlie and her dad had left, Laura wrapped Holly in her arms and squeezed her tight. She breathed in the clean smell of shampoo and chlorine from her daughter's hair. 'I promise to be a better mum from now on, Holly. Once we get Poppy safely home where she belongs, it will be us three against the world.'

'And the kittens?' Smiled Holly. 'Of course!' agreed her mum.

The hospital staff had gently insisted, late the previous evening, that Laura was to go home and rest, having been at her daughter's side for over twenty-four hours. Poppy was being well looked after and had needed to recuperate after her traumatic experience, plus the thorough and invasive process she had gone through for the police. Instead of going straight home though, Laura had gone to the large supermarket near the hospital and had done a much needed and well overdue shop. Not only stocking up on the basics and cupboard fillers, but also adding luxuries and treats for the girls. Once home and unpacked, she'd scrubbed the house from top to bottom, changing all the bed linen and vacuuming each room and then, determinedly, she had flushed her remaining stash down the toilet as well as emptying out the remaining wine bottles left in the wine rack. As she had said to Jonny, she knew that she had to get a grip of herself to be able to be there to support her children.

After lunch, the two of them went upstairs together and chose an outfit for Poppy to come home in. Laura felt nostalgic and told Holly the much-loved story of bringing them both home from hospital when they had been born. Holly knew her own birth story well but always loved to hear how her dad and six-year-old Poppy had jokingly battled it out with water pistols to be the first to hold her.

As they left for the journey to the hospital, Holly thought she saw the notorious red car lurking at the end of the road just past their house. Deciding it would not be a good idea to risk her mum's mood deteriorating, she kept the information to herself. After a few miles, Holly couldn't see it following them any more so she figured it could have been in her imagination anyway and was glad she had not spoken up.

The noise and bustle as they walked through the hospital meant they didn't talk much, especially as they stood right to the back in the lift to make space for the chirpy, young porter and the very sick looking lady in the bed he was pushing. Holly could hear the tinny music leaking out from the headphones he had dangling by his neck. She smiled back at him when he caught her eye, winked at her then he turned back to his patient and murmured comfortingly. Laura looked down at Holly and squeezed her hand then they stepped out of the lift together, edging past the large, wheeled bed.

Poppy had been given a side room on the paediatric ward and once they had been buzzed through the secure door entry system, Holly raced to find her sister. She had a vague recollection of knowing the way round, as she had spent a few nights there herself, a few years ago, being investigated for unexplained stomach pain.

Poppy looked up as Holly entered her room with her mother not far behind. She looked a lot better than last time Holly had seen her two days previously. There was still a slight haunted look in her eyes though. With her left arm in a sling and the visible bruising glowing on her jaw, she would obviously need a lot of looking after at home. The doctors hoped that with her arm immobilised and held in the correct position, her clavicle bone would be able to reknit itself together without the need for an operation. Laura carefully hugged her injured daughter. She struggled to swallow back the gut-wrenching emotion that engulfed her every time she saw what had been done to her first born. Her baby!

The nursing Sister knocked on the door as she joined them in the private room. She perched at the side of Poppy and lifted her good arm to perform the last set of observations before she was to be discharged. 'Your blood pressure is still a bit on the high side, Duckie, but that's to be expected, what with the shock you've had.' Poppy just stared at the wall behind Holly's head. She had not said a word since any of them had entered the room. The nurse explained the pain medication dosage and reminded

Laura that they would be sent an appointment in a few weeks for an outpatient check-up. Glancing at Holly, to check she wasn't paying too much attention, she also handed Laura several leaflets offering trauma counselling and therapy.

The three of them all helped to get the silent teenager dressed and into her trainers. Holly chattered constantly to Poppy while she bent down to tie her sister's shoelaces. Hearing about what the kittens had been up to led to silent tears rolling down Poppy's cheeks but, although she didn't speak, she did reach out and stroke Holly's hair.

As they gathered up all their belongings and left the room, the experienced nurse put her hand on Laura's arm. 'It will take time,' she said. 'The physical trauma will heal faster than the memories and flashbacks.' Laura nodded sadly in response and led her precious girls back out through the hospital towards the carpark. Holly was determined not to moan about the heaviness of the bag she was carrying. When she stopped to hump the strap back onto her shoulder, she fell slightly behind the others. Thinking that she saw the same red car lurking by the ticket machine, she quickened her pace and hurried to get into the safety of her mum's car. Maybe she was just being paranoid!

They spent the rest of the afternoon chilling on the large sofas in the front room. Holly helped to make toffee popcorn, then they all sat watching some of their favourite family films. Poppy was quiet but seemed content enough as she stroked Shady who was curled on her lap. Holly was very glad to have her sister home. Hopefully, now that Poppy clearly wouldn't want to be friends with the horrible men anymore, they might be able to have family time more often. It had actually been a long time since the three of them had spent an afternoon hanging out, all in the same room!

Chapter 8

Mrs Redleigh and Mr George were called into an early meeting with the headteacher first thing on the Monday morning. The police, school, social workers and highly qualified and experienced counsellors would all be working together to keep everyone involved safe. There was also the concern that the Press would get wind of the pupils' identities, so an emergency safe-guarding plan was being put into place. Arasuli had the additional trauma of having lost his home so he would need extra support too.

Because the meeting had over-run, it was Mr George who was outside that morning to lead Summer Class into school. He smiled and hi-fived all the children in the class as they pretended not to jostle each other in the line. 'Walk this way!' he called, setting off through the school marching and occasionally jumping up in various positions. The children giggled with delight as they copied his actions.

Mrs Redleigh was just finishing writing up Bertie's large weekly visual timetable but she stopped to greet her class as they trooped in and took their seats ready for the morning activities. 'No Arasuli today?' she observed quietly to her TA. He shook his head.

Holly noticed the empty seat next to Louise too. She put her hand up. 'Please Mrs Redleigh, can I sit next to Louise today?' Most of the class stopped to listen to the answer. Mrs Redleigh never let anyone move seats! Holly was very surprised when her teacher nodded. 'Just until assembly.' Holly ignored the sly, muttered comments from Polly and Ola as she moved her pencil case to the front of the class and sat down.

Although Louise was happy to have her friend next to her, she was also aware Bertie was put out that his friend wasn't in school. She could sense his agitation from across the classroom. Every morning whilst they all came in quietly and got on with the activities on the tables, Mrs Redleigh would sit with him and go through his daily timetable. He didn't seem to be listening to her though and was rocking backwards and forwards.

Holly nudged Louise. 'I thought you weren't going to be here on Friday?'

Glancing at the weekly planner, Louise nodded and put up her hand. 'Mrs Redleigh, don't forget me and Bertie won't be here on Friday as we are going to London.'

'Ah yes, thanks, Louise,' she replied. Because it had been such a stressful morning already, Mrs Redleigh had forgotten the Housten twins had the day booked off to travel up for their next modelling shoot.

During break, Holly, Louise and Otterlie huddled together on the grass. With only a week to go until half term, the area they sat on would soon be out of bounds, so they decided to make the most of it before the weather changed. They hadn't all been together since Friday night. Holly sighed and began to pick at the daisies. She felt glad to be at school. It made her feel things were normal. Otterlie animatedly began telling Louise about the diving board and Holly winced. She knew that Louise would get jealous for not having been part of the experience. She was right. 'Well, I would have dived straight off,' Louise stated. 'Only babies jump!'

Otterlie looked hurt but before she could respond, Holly handed each of them a daisy chain necklace she had made. 'Friends forever?' The awkward moment was forgotten, and the girls jumped up, twirling around to show off their new accessories.

When the whistle blew, they ran to join the line, gathering up Bertie on the way. He had been standing alone by the wall watching some Year Three children playing football. It seemed that the mean girls, Isla, Polly and Esther had now recruited Ola into their gang. A low chant of "Holly Hippo is fat and wet, that's because she's the teacher's pet..." could be heard as they walked past. Some of the boys in the class had heard too and were snickering but were not actually joining in the taunts.

Before she even had time to react herself, Holly saw the blur of Otterlie fly past her. She watched in disbelief as her tiny but fiery friend launched herself onto the back of the ringleader, Isla, taking them both down to the ground. A expectant hush crept over the whole playground. Otterlie had only lost her temper once before in school, when she'd been in Year Four, and that had resulted in the offending boy losing his front teeth. This time though, she was now sat on the bully with her hands grabbing the sobbing girl's hair. Yanking her head backwards and forward with every word she announced through gritted teeth, 'If... you... ever... ever... pick on... anyone... especially my friend... I will hurt you bad!' Before anything else could be said, the three teachers on playground duty pulled the girls apart and Holly watched as her friend was marched off to the office. Snivelling, Isla was taken to the medical room to be checked over. Although she was worried that Otterlie was about to get into big trouble, a warm feeling settled over Holly. Her friend had totally stuck up for her! Esther, Polly and Ola didn't seem so scary now. They had got into their places in the line and kept nervously looking around, obviously feeling a bit guilty about their involvement. Louise winked at her.

Mrs Redleigh was not impressed to hear about what had happened and she gave the whole class a lecture on the school rules. Holly had not dared to go back to sit next to Louise, but the two of them still managed to make eye contact to acknowledge how their teacher had looked towards the mean girls when talking about how bullying was totally unacceptable!

Just before lunch the headteacher, Mrs Rose, came to the classroom door and beckoned to Mr George. Holly saw them look towards her and Louise when they spoke to each other and a bad feeling squirmed inside her. Otterlie still hadn't returned to the classroom, even after Isla had shuffled in looking sorry for herself. Mr George whispered to Mrs Redleigh, who nodded but then carried on with her explanation of life in Victorian England. He asked Holly and Louise to follow him quietly out of the classroom towards the front office. 'Nothing to worry about, girls,' he reassured, seeing the fear on Holly's face, 'The Police are here and just want to go through your statements to check they haven't missed anything about what you witnessed at the weekend.'

'Where's Otterlie? Has she been expelled?' asked Louise.

'Of course she hasn't,' answered the headteacher who had waited for them further down the corridor, 'We had a chat but she's fine and waiting to go and meet the police officers with you two.'

Holly hugged Otterlie before all three sat huddled up on the large comfy sofa in the office. Because she was sandwiched between her friends, Holly reached out and held both their hands. She could see that Otterlie had been crying. 'You were awesome.

Isla didn't even know what was going on when you ran at her!'
Otterlie gave a watery smile in response to Holly's whispered
comment but they all fell silent as just then the door opened and
Mr George led two plain-clothed officers into the room. Jonny,
Laura and Claudette followed them in. They had to be present
whilst the girls were talking to the Officers. After hugging their
children, they perched on hard-backed chairs in the corner of the
room, leaving the girls snuggled together on the sofa.

When the girls had finished confirming their description of
the men they had seen on Friday, they said goodbye to their
parents. They were allowed to take their lunch boxes and eat in
the library as they had missed normal lunch break. Holly knew
this was also to keep them away from Isla because she heard the
adults talking conspiringly as they walked past. Considering the
seemingly stressful morning they'd had, the girls were actually
in good spirits as they sprawled in the beanbags and chattered
whilst they shared their crisps. Louise even allowed herself to
have a couple, although she made her friends promise to not tell
Bertie or her mum! Holly was still slightly in awe of Otterlie who
hadn't got away scot-free with her outburst; she had been put on
litter picking duty for the next two days so would lose her
morning break.

Poppy was in the car when Laura came back to collect Holly
at the end of the day. She'd had the week off college to recover
so had spent the day at home with her mum who had also
cancelled her event-planning schedule to look after her daughter.
Holly threw her bags onto the back seat. Before clambering in,
she impulsively gave her big sister a loving kiss on the head.

Mrs Redleigh was still talking to Otterlie's dad, who was, in
turn, glancing furiously towards Isla, but she had gesticulated to
Laura that she would like a quick word too. 'Uh oh, Hols, what

have you done?' Poppy asked. Holly shrugged but told her sister how Otterlie had stuck up for her against the mean girls. Hearing Poppy laugh as she listened to the embellished recap gave Holly a warm feeling. She'd been worried that Poppy was broken and would be stuck looking sad forever.

On the drive home Laura looked pensive. She took a deep breath. 'I'm so, so sorry, girls. I didn't realise you were both dealing with so much.' A stray tear rolled desolately down her cheek which she quickly wiped away. 'If those girls are horrible to you again, Holly, please will you tell me? I will not have anyone hurting my babies anymore!'

Holly nodded. 'It's okay, Mum, I'm all right. Besides I have a new secret weapon. Lucie, Polly's twin, but she's the nice one, told us this afternoon that all the mean girls are in big trouble for bullying because lots of others in the class had told on them too. Lucie also said that Isla had been laughed at for letting tiny Otterlie deck her and now nobody was scared of her anymore!' Laura looked less upset upon hearing this but she still kept her hand on Poppy's knee, as if to let her know how sorry she was for not being there.

They had another family evening. Holly felt a lot less lonely at home, now that both her mum and sister were physically and emotionally present in the house. The mood was still subdued. Poppy often was found just staring into space, but at least they were all together and there was food in the fridge which encouraged them to all work alongside each other to cook up a feast. Holly spoke to the smart speaker and uplifting dance music filled the kitchen. Poppy even managed a one-armed dance with her little sister, spinning her towards Laura who took over and sashayed the girls around the room. They were interrupted by the phone ringing. Seeing it was Claudette calling, Laura took the phone and left the kitchen, closing the door behind her.

In the pause when the song finished, the sisters looked at each other as they heard Laura's voice being carried through the open window. 'Thank you for letting me know, yes, yes, I agree, as you say every cloud... Okay we'll speak when you're back from London, please thank Stephen again, oh I know, if he hadn't been there...' The quiet opening of the next song suddenly built up to the crescendo and the girls could no longer hear the conversation.

When she returned to the kitchen the girls had laid the fajita options out on the large table and were sat quietly, sipping their drinks whilst they waited. Laura looked at their expectant faces. She could see the worrying look in Poppy's eyes as they searched her face questionably. She smiled at her daughters.

'Claudette was just letting us know that Arasuli and his uncle have been given a room in a B and B. She said that they didn't even have a proper room before and were just sleeping in an outbuilding behind the shops, with no heating or windows.'

'Cool!' answered Holly. 'I loved the B and B we stayed at in Greece last year.'

Although Poppy looked at her mother, neither of them decided to say anything to Holly to shatter her mental image of the accommodation the Deebs would be moving into. Poppy's friend had gone into temporary housing the previous year and, when they had popped in to collect a jumper before going to the park, the landlady had taken it upon herself to roughly search the teenagers, helping herself to a few pounds from the bottom of Poppy's bag. Indignant, she had started to make a fuss but had been led away by her friend who had said they would have the power cut off in their room again if they complained.

Chapter 9

Otterlie

I can see the flicker of the rotating nightlight through my eyelids before I actually fully open my eyes. It creates planet images on the ceiling and I love it. Knowing I won't be able to go back to sleep now, I decide to get up. My alarm clock hasn't yet beeped but it feels like it's morning so it means I'll have time to rearrange my teddy shelf before breakfast!

I knew that most people in my class were going to be excited that it was the last day before we had a week off, but I was dreading it. Ever since Aimee had married my dad last year and moved into our house with her son, Elliot had been picking on me and trying to get me in trouble. He normally spent half the time at his dad's house, but his dad was going away for work so I would have to put up with him for the whole of half term. Elliot had turned sixteen last month and he's tall and strong and in Year Eleven at the big school in the city. I've got ages until I'm even ten and my dad always says that I'm small for my age too. Hopefully today will be all right though as I've already got dressed in my uniform and snuck downstairs, past his closed bedroom door, without hearing him. I nearly jump out of my skin when the kitchen door opens with a creak, but luckily, it's Dad.

Otterlie grinned as Jonny suddenly picked her up and swung her into the kitchen, sitting her on the breakfast bar. 'Morning

LeeLee, it's Friday! And guess what?'

Otterlie just looked at him questionably as he continued, 'Tonight, it's just you and me. Aimee is taking Elliot to the cinema, the film they are watching is a fifteen though so you're too pipsqueak to go, we could go somewhere else though if you like…' He paused to look in his wallet, which did not seem to make him happy. 'No, Dad,' replied Otterlie. 'Please can we just stay in and have fun, just us?'

Aimee joined them in the kitchen. She pulled Otterlie gently onto the floor then, as Jonny flicked on the radio, she spun her round, then pulled her over to the large, sagging navy sofa and began to neaten the corn rows that she had painstakingly done the evening before. Otterlie saw her dad smile gratefully at his wife. She knew he struggled to do her hair and when she was younger, she often had been left with a wild halo of untamed but beautiful fuzz.

Hearing a bang from upstairs, Otterlie flicked her brown eyes towards the closed, kitchen door but breathed out a sigh of relief when it remained shut and no footsteps were heard on the stairs either. This morning was going well so far because there had been no sign of her stepbrother! As if reading her thoughts, Aimee reminded them both that Elliot had an inset day, so she had no urgent need to wake him up.

Kissing his daughter and wife goodbye, Jonny headed off to work, leaving the women in his life to finish their toast while they sat together watching early morning television.

School was uneventful that day. Otterlie and Holly did not even hear so much as a vicious word from Isla and her gang. They were all on warnings from Mrs Redleigh, so were on their best behaviour.

Louise and Bertie were absent as they were on their way to

London for their new modelling contract. During whole school assembly, Otterlie whispered to Holly that she had heard Mr George and Mrs Redleigh chatting about Arasuli, saying that the reason he hadn't been in school all week was because some amazing information had been unearthed by his newly appointed social worker. Not able to discuss it during assembly, because of risk of detention with the headteacher, the two girls spent their break time speculating about what it could be. Although they came up with some crazy theories, they knew they would have to wait until they saw him again to find out.

Summer Class teamed up with the Year Six (Blossom) class, and they all had a whole afternoon of netball practice, in preparation for the county tournament that was to be hosted at a local school a few weeks after half term. Otterlie had been chosen to play Centre, because although she was small, she was fast and able to jump exceptionally high to get the ball. Mr George often told her she was Year Five's greatest asset which gave her a warm feeling inside. Although she would never admit it to Holly, she felt secretly pleased that Louise wasn't there because she often made her feel guilty for being good at sports. Otterlie knew that this was because her friend liked to be the one who was the best at everything and Louise's long legs and height meant she was often the obvious choice when teams were being picked, but Mr George had quickly spotted the previously hidden talent in Otterlie.

Typically, the dark clouds that had been lurking all afternoon decided that they would choose the exact moment the bell went for the end of the day to release their downpour over Mimosa Primary. As Otterlie and Holly ran across the playground towards the waiting adults at the gates, the rain splashed up their legs, drenching them. Laughing, Otterlie said goodbye as Holly scrambled into her car where Laura was holding open the door. 'Have a lovely half term. Say hi to your dad and Aimee from me,' called Holly's mum.

When Otterlie jumped into the back of Aimee's car, her stepmum didn't seem to notice that, as she turned her head to reverse, Elliot choose that moment to adjust his seat in the front, slamming it back with force into Otterlie's legs. She glared at him but did not react. She had learnt from experience, that if she complained to her dad or Aimee and consequently, he was spoken to, he would then take it out on her much worse later when he could corner her on her own. She slid over to the seat behind Aimee and looked out of the window as she refused to give him the satisfaction of knowing that he had hurt her. Aimee was so nice and made her dad so happy. Otterlie just wished Elliot wasn't part of the package!

She stood dripping wet in the kitchen, letting Aimee remove her sodden uniform to put straight into the washing machine. When the fresh, angry bruise on her leg was noticed, Otterlie mumbled about being on the netball team in answer to the enquiry on how she had got the injury. She could feel the heat of Elliot's glare burning into the back of her head. She knew he must have been satisfied with her answer though as his footsteps then continued up the stairs.

Aimee handed Otterlie her spotty dressing gown and gave her a big snuggle. 'Love you, LeeLee,' she said, adopting the pet name that her husband called his daughter. Otterlie returned the squeeze. She really did love her stepmum too.

When Jonny arrived home, he took off his dirty overalls and threw them into the semi-loaded washing machine while Otterlie held open the door for him. She loved the comforting smell of oil and grease which clung to her dad's work gear. He turned on the quick wash cycle then enveloped them both into his arms. 'What more could a man need in his life?'

Grinning, Aimee and Otterlie rolled their eyes. 'Food!' they chorused. They all had the same conversation every day. Aimee called up to Elliot and Jonny hi-fived him as he joined them at the kitchen table. It was a bit of a squeeze but cosy and they all sat around chatting whilst eating the chicken curry that Aimee had prepared. The Eminem and Rihanna duet came on the radio and Otterlie stood up to turn up the volume and then rapped and sang along to the lyrics flawlessly. Even Elliot failed to hide how impressed he was at her being word and pitch perfect! 'Way to go, kid, that was awesome.' Otterlie beamed. Praise from Elliot was usually unheard of.

All four of them performed their usual, daily, choreographed routine of cleaning the dishes away and loading the dishwasher then Aimee and Elliot left to drive into the city.

Otterlie felt an unexpected sense of pride as she snuggled up with her dad to watch an animated film on the sofa that evening. She had been praised for her talents in both netball and rapping that day. They sat together, half-heartedly watching the screen but discussing their respective days too. Suddenly, her stomach gave a large leap of realisation in response to her dad's reaction to her news that she was going to be playing netball in the county tournaments. He had just said that he thought he had a photo of her mum somewhere, dressed in netball kit. She gaped at him in astonishment.

She had spent her whole life thinking her dad did not know anything about her mum and now she had been given a new titbit of information.

Chapter 10

It was the first thought to enter her head when she awoke the next day; her mum had once played netball. Her dad had promised he would look for the photograph that evening when he finished work.

As usual, on a Saturday morning, Otterlie had to amuse herself while Aimee worked from home. There were strict, unspoken instructions to not go out to the converted outbuilding at the end of the garden, which was Aimee's hairdressing salon, unless there was uncontrollable blood or broken bones involved!

Not wanting to disturb Elliot, who she could hear playing some kind of loud, shooting game on his Xbox, she lay on her bed with her sketch pad, doodling images of what she thought her mum looked like. When she tired of this, she emptied out her Lego chest and began to build an intricate castle. Totally absorbed, she failed to notice the muting of the tinny gunfire from the room next to hers.

When Elliot had finished in the bathroom, he stopped to look in on Otterlie. Being sixteen, he was expected by his mum and Jonny to watch her when they were both working. Almost without thinking he walked into her room to look at her construction, he then flicked his foot forward and knocked over the structure. 'Whoops,' he said, a slight flash of remorse registering on his face, before he turned and walked back to his own, smaller bedroom.

The rage boiled up from Otterlie's stomach. She could feel

it vibrating through her veins. Letting out a blood-curdling scream she jumped up and ran after her stepbrother. Catching up with him in his doorway, she threw herself at his back; punching and kicking with all her strength. Elliot yelped as her fist connected with his nose. Ignoring the blood that began to trickle down his face, he picked her up and dumped her in the hallway before slamming the door and retreating to his room. Still fuming, Otterlie stormed into the bathroom and grabbed his toothbrush from the cup holder.

Muttering to herself, she used one hand to wipe away the angry tears dripping from her nose and with the other hand she furiously scrubbed the toilet with Elliot's toothbrush. Finally, spent of emotion, she slunk back to lie on her bed, stepping over the ruined tower.

It didn't take long for the anger to fade. As Otterlie's heavy breathing began to subside, she suddenly felt a wave of panic. What if she made Elliot really sick? What if he died from the germs in the toilet? She opened her door quietly and snuck back into the bathroom. Removing the violated toothbrush from the holder again, she snuck downstairs and buried it deep inside the kitchen bin.

When Aimee returned to the house at lunch time, she found both children sitting in the lounge together watching a film. Although subdued, they seemed happy in each other's company, so she left them to finish what they were watching whilst she went to make lunch. 'Grub's up!' she called a little while later. Nobody spoke much as they ate the ham and cheese sandwiches that Aimee had prepared.

Otterlie glanced a few times towards the bin, feeling awful for what she had done but hoping her actions would go undiscovered. It seemed that Elliot must be feeling bad about ruining her castle too as he had not mentioned the fact she had given him a nosebleed. He had joined her on the sofa about forty minutes before he knew his mum would be back in from the salon and they had both managed a weak smile at each other before pretending to be engrossed in the television.

Elliot stayed at home in the afternoon but Otterlie opted to go shopping with Aimee. As they trudged around the supermarket, Otterlie asked the question that had been on her mind since the day before, 'Aimee, do you really think Dad knows lots about my mum? He said that she played netball like me but before he always told me that he didn't know much about her!'

Aimee smiled at her eager stepdaughter. She and Jonny had talked late into the night about his omission with the netball information and had decided to talk to her together, honestly, when he got home from work. 'Be patient, LeeLee, he will tell you everything we know later. You are old enough to understand more now.'

Realising that she would not get any more information, Otterlie dropped the subject. She snuck a new toothbrush into the shopping trolley for Elliot as they went down the toiletries aisle. When they were at the checkout Otterlie held her breath but her addition to the week's shopping went unnoticed, much to her relief.

As a treat, Jonny ordered takeaway pizza for their dinner that evening. Normally, Otterlie would be extremely excited about this but she was more focused on the small shoe box that her dad had fetched from the loft. When the pizza arrived, Elliot asked to take his through into the lounge. He stated that he did not need to be part of the discussion. Nobody argued with him, so he took himself off quite happily to watch another few episodes in his latest series.

Otterlie was fidgety with apprehension. Sensing this, Jonny pushed a slice of pizza towards her then sat down next to her at the kitchen table. 'Do you want me to stay?' asked Aimee.

'Of course, Love,' smiled Jonny. He took a deep breath and turned towards the expectant face of his daughter. 'Otterlie, I met your mum in a dance club one night. I was there after work with a few friends and we had all had a few too many beers to drink.' He paused to look at Aimee. She nodded encouragingly so he continued, 'Your mum was on the dance floor. She was exotic and beautiful, just like you, and I couldn't believe my luck when she seemed to fancy me too! At the end of the night, I invited her back to my house. I shared a house with three other guys back then, but she didn't seem to mind. In fact, I remember her commenting on how tidy she thought it was for a man pad. Anyway, the next morning when I woke up, she had gone! All I knew was that her name was Ebony.' As he paused, Otterlie tried out the name for herself. 'Ebony,' she said out loud. Her mum was called Ebony!

They all spent a few minutes digesting the information and enjoying the pizza, then Aimee prodded her husband to finish the story. Otterlie paused her chewing to listen, agog, to her dad. 'I felt sad for a while,' admitted Jonny. 'She had left without saying goodbye and I had no way to contact her. Of course, I tried to look her up on social media, but I had no idea of her last name.' He took a large slug of the beer in front of him then carried on,

'It was just over a year later that I saw her again...' Otterlie gulped down her pizza, she felt like she had been waiting her whole life for this sacred information. She listened intently to her dad as he continued, 'It was the day after my twenty-second birthday, middle of June. I was still in bed when I heard the knocking on the front door. I remember putting the pillow over my head to try and ignore it, but then my bedroom door opened and Holly's dad, Marcus, was standing there telling me to get up. I had known him for years and his brother was one of my house mates so he'd been invited out with us the night before to celebrate my birthday. Anyway, Marcus made me go downstairs and Ebony was there in the lounge and she was holding you! You were three months old, but you were still tiny to me. I had never held a baby before, but Ebony just handed you to me with a bag and then she left, saying she would come back in an hour. I was scared I would drop you, but Marcus was a dad. He already had Poppy and Holly, so he showed me what to do.'

Jonny paused again. Aimee could see this was hard for him to recount so she sat down next to him and then reached across the table to grasp Otterlie's hands.

Feeling overwhelmed, Otterlie stood up shakily and found herself pulled into a three-way cuddle. It was a lot to digest. She buried her head into the comfort of her dad's chest and asked, 'So was that it, did she just dump me with you?' She felt, rather than saw, the shake of her father's head in response.

'No, she came back with a letter for me. It was very emotional. It explained that she soon had to move to St Lucia to take care of her sick mother and there was no way she could take you with her. Her family were devout people, deeply religious, and would not accept her if she arrived with a baby born out of wedlock. It would have brought shame on her family. I got the impression they were extremely strict with her. From the moment she turned up at my door with you, she had decided that you needed to be raised in this country, by me; your father. There was no changing her mind. Over the next few months, you stayed with me and my housemates. Marcus and Laura would come round as often as they could to help me adjust to your routine. Because Holly was a few months older than you, they gave me lots of clothes and other bits that she no longer needed.'

'But did she just not want me anymore?' Otterlie murmured, the emotion thick in her voice.

Not knowing how to answer that, Jonny continued with the facts, 'I saw Ebony again when she met me the day before she flew. By then, we had changed your birth certificate to include my name, so I had parental responsibility, and Ebony had legally signed over custody to me. She knew she would not be coming back, and she begged me to never contact her in her new life. As a parting gift to us both she handed me a set of keys. Otterlie, your mum used every penny of her savings to buy us this house. She wanted you to have a stable home. When we moved in, the house was empty except for this shoebox.'

He pulled the box on the table towards them and detangled Otterlie from around his neck. Gingerly, she opened the lid. Inside there were five photos, four of Ebony, including her about twelve-years-old playing netball, and one of Otterlie as a new-born baby. Lifting them out as delicately as if they were made from glass, Otterlie lay them carefully on the table.

Aimee pulled Jonny up and led him out of the room to leave Otterlie in peace to absorb the pictures. Otterlie heard her stepmum reassure her dad that he had done a great job, but she was too distracted by the photos to listen to his response.

Chapter 11

Otterlie was not sure if Elliot had been warned by his mum to be nice to her, or if it was because of what had happened with the Lego, but she felt almost wary of him. It seemed he was ignoring her and not trying to wind her up. At least when he was consistently mean she knew what to expect. He had even saved her the last of her favourite cereal at breakfast time!

After lunch on the Monday, Holly's mum called to speak to Aimee. Although she could only hear one side of the lengthy conversation, Otterlie could tell that the adults were talking about the girls and how trauma affected them. Bored, she wandered into the garden. She sat on the tyre swing that her dad and Elliot had hung from the branch of an enormous tree that overhung their garden. When the call ended and Aimee shared the request from Laura, Otterlie jumped up and down with excitement. She had been asked to go into Holly's house each day to look after Rufus and Shady, the cats. Aimee explained that Laura was taking Poppy and Holly away for a few days to visit their grandparents in Wales.

Otterlie was disappointed that both of her best friends were not going to be at home during half term. Louise and Bertie were going to be staying in London all week having their photos taken for a new advertising campaign and now she knew that Holly would be away too. Her own time off from school would be spent closer to home. She knew Aimee didn't have to work on

Mondays, but the rest of the week she would have to go to work with her dad. This was not a bad thing. The large garage where he had set up his own mechanic business was always busy and sometimes Otterlie was even allowed to answer the phone or help pass tools to her dad when he was under a customer's car.

For the rest of the afternoon, Otterlie played on the grass outside the front of her row of houses. Ruby, Ewan and Harry from her class all lived on her road too and the four of them played together, setting up an elaborate game of It with lots of extra rules which kept changing. She thought about telling them about her mum, but in the end, she chose to keep her newly discovered family history to herself. Instead, she taught Ewan how to rap. He picked it up quite quickly but admitted to his peers that there was no way his mum would let him listen to music like that at home. He came from a family of practicing Jehovah's Witnesses. Otterlie had asked him what that meant once, but she had only fixated on what he had told her about having presents any time of the year, not just at birthdays and Christmas like she did, and she had thought that was really cool!

Otterlie really enjoyed her half term holiday. Every day after helping her dad at work, they went to Holly's house to feed and play with the kittens. They had grown so much already and were full of energy. Jonny would pretend to shriek and leap in the air dramatically as they would often spring for his toes. She hadn't managed to convince him to allow her to have one of her own yet, but she was working on it.

On the Friday evening, a few hours before Laura and the girls were due home, Otterlie posted the spare key back through the letter box and skipped down the drive to where her dad was waiting by the van. He'd gone on ahead to make a work call. Realising he was still busy, she walked past him and headed towards a grassy verge to practise her cartwheels. Abruptly, her heart skipped a beat and she felt an unfamiliar sense of fear gnaw at her insides. The red car with two of the scary men in it was parked, slightly hidden under some trees, just across the road. Frozen to the spot, she was close enough to watch the realisation dawn in their eyes. She knew they recognised her. As the passenger door opened and the man began to haul his large bulk into a standing position, Otterlie found her voice, 'Daaaaaaddddd, Daaaaaddddd.' Parental instinct propelled Jonny at a superhuman speed towards the sound of pure terror which quivered in his daughter's voice.

Chapter 12

Otterlie still felt the aftermath of the adrenalin comedown a few hours later and she sat cuddled up, on the reassuringly familiar sofa, between her dad and Aimee. She looked down at her hands, over which she didn't seem to have control any more. They were moving shakily. A weird sensation she had never experienced before.

Aimee noticed and placed her own hands over the top then gently lowered them into Otterlie's lap.

'We won't be much longer, I promise,' reassured the older of the two female police officers who had been going through their statements again. 'Are you sure you don't require medical attention for your hand?' she asked the question for a third time to Jonny who was still holding the frozen peas, wrapped in a flowery tea towel, on his knuckles.

'No. No, I'm fine,' he muttered. Seeing his wife raise her eyebrows at him questionably and nod her head towards his daughter he added more confidently, 'Will this go against the case?'

'Not at all. In fact it will strengthen it. I very much doubt that Mr Karver will proceed with pressing charges against you for assault, even though you did do a nice number on his face.' She paused to look at her colleague who shrugged conspiringly. 'You were defending your daughter and, thanks to Laura Rivers' state of the art camera system, which includes audio, we have the whole exchange recorded, which will be used in court. The fact that you happen to be an amateur boxer just means we will have to retake his mugshot to show his new shape nose!'

The officers stood up to leave. 'Don't worry, they will not be released on bail again. We found enough evidence in their car to suggest their intentions for being outside the Rivers' residence were definitely not honourable.'

Jonny remembered his manners and jumped up to show them out. As he left the kitchen, Otterlie folded herself into the loving embrace from her stepmother and let go of the tsunami of emotion that had been building up inside her.

The memory images flashed inside her head like scenes from a film. She recalled the smell of body odour from the vile man as he had lurched forward and grabbed her wrist. He had been muttering to his equally scruffy mate that she would be their insurance policy, although she still didn't know what they had meant by that. Subconsciously, she rubbed her wrist where a circle of finger shaped bruises had formed.

As she had been yanked towards the car, her hero father had appeared, flooring the man with one punch before propelling her back towards Holly's driveway. She had followed his command to get in the van and lock the doors, running into the driveway and not looking back.

When her dad had reappeared in the driveway not long after, his feet crunching on the gravel as he sped towards his daughter in the van, he hadn't spoken, just hugged her tightly then driven them out onto the road to wait for the police. Otterlie had dared to look towards the red car and seen the two men writhing and lying on the floor. She glanced at her dad's hands to confirm. She had been right in her assumption. He had hurt them to save her.

Even now, as the sobs still wracked her body, she felt the fierce love surge in her heart for her dad.

Fear sliced through her again as the image of the men trying to get to their feet as the police had arrived entered her memories. She had seen the venomous look on their faces as they were handcuffed.

Just then, Jonny came back into the kitchen. He clocked the situation and rushed over to console Otterlie. Aimee subtly detangled herself and went to find Elliot who had been banished upstairs in the commotion but now deserved to be filled in on the evening's events. Jonny wrapped his arms around Otterlie and held her tight until her heaving anguish subsided.

The next evening, the four of them sat watching Saturday evening television together. Elliot was being quite funny, copying the mishaps of the contenders and imitating the canned laughter of the audience. He changed the channel just in time to catch a theme tune that was playing, announcing that the search for the next talented individual or group was about to begin. Just before Otterlie had time to get excited and suggest she should apply with her rapping skills, the phone rang. The adults glanced at each other. Aimee looked at her son pleadingly. Remembering the request she had made of him earlier in the day, he looked at his stepsister. 'Come on, Buttface,' he said affectionally. He had admitted to his mum that he felt more protective of her after everything that had happened lately. 'We are going to watch this in my room.' Otterlie looked at him in disbelief but her dad was shooing her out of the room as he clicked to answer the call. She didn't have a choice but to follow Elliot up the stairs.

She hovered on the stairs, trying to work out what was so secretive about the phone call but before she could deduce much more than it was Laura on the other end of the line, Aimee firmly closed the door and she could hear nothing more than the rise and fall of muffled voices. Defeated, she scampered up the remaining few stairs. She thought about just going into her own room but Elliot was standing in his doorway, waiting expectantly.

As Elliot jumped onto his bed next to her, she flinched. His fist was coming towards her. Bracing for the impact she closed her eyes. Surprised when there was no pain, Otterlie dared to open one eye. She was just in time to see and feel the light-hearted punch connect with her shoulder. Confused, Otterlie decided to ask the question burning the tip of her tongue, 'Why are you not being horrible to me, Elliot?'

He looked pensive for a few seconds then pushed her over and pretended to fart on her leg. 'Maybe I realised you aren't as bad and annoying as I thought!' He grinned at her then continued, 'But don't worry, I'm sure you will irritate me again soon. Are we gonna watch this talent show or not?' He gestured to his monitor. When Otterlie just shrugged he grinned again. 'Perfect, you can sit there and tell me when you see the enemy coming up behind me.' Chucking her a spare headset, he loaded his favourite shooting game and began to play. Although she was technically being ignored, Otterlie felt very privileged to be harmoniously sitting next to her stepbrother.

Chapter 13

The half term had passed in a blur for Mr Thomas George. He loved his job at Mimosa Primary but unfortunately the salary of a Teaching Assistant was never going to get his bank account very far out of his overdraft. Consequently, he still rented the spare room at his mother's house and had a second job at a supermarket to enable him to try and build up some savings. Having worked there for most of the last week, he was thinking about the awkward conversation with the manager he'd had the day before. Brooding over the fact his hours were going to be cut again to just a twelve-hour shift on a Saturday was the reason he was distracted and failed to register the commotion going on around him. He had to screech his bike to a halt as he rode up to the gates of Mimosa on the Monday morning. Although it was before eight a.m., anxious parents were already congregating. They were speculating over the very high police presence, blue lighting through the village, since early that morning.

Otterlie stood with Aimee waiting to go through the gates. She watched Mr George being ushered into the main entrance by Mrs Redleigh and wondered what they were talking about. She was aware enough to understand that something was going on locally and realised it was probably something to do with the bad men. Unusually, Mrs Rose, the headteacher, was walking towards the main gates. Instead of opening them wide to allow the waiting children to swarm in, she just opened the smaller, side gate and began ushering them in a few at a time. Her eyes were surreptitiously darting up and down the road. Aimee kissed

Otterlie's head then propelled her forward.

Once on the playground, the normal chattering and bustle of familiarity relaxed Otterlie. Ewan grinned as he rushed past her then stopped to retreat and rapped out a good morning greeting. He had obviously been working on his deliverance and it was surprisingly good. Louise and Bertie suddenly appeared and true to form Louise launched into a torrent of excited chatter, describing her amazing week in London. As she listened to tales of modelling antics, Otterlie glanced at Bertie. She could see him scanning the playground for his friend. The apprehension was causing him to flap his hands anxiously. Louise noticed too but, before she could placate her brother, Arasuli and Holly could be seen strolling towards them across the playground.

The relief was immediately obvious on Bertie's face. He rocked back and forth on the balls of his feet while he waited for his friend. Otterlie had not seen Arasuli since the night when they had rescued Holly's sister but today, he looked really well. She thought that, uncharacteristically, he looked neater, as if someone had ironed his school uniform like Aimee often did for her. Leaving the boys to their own reunion, the three best friends embraced in a group hug. Holly handed them both pink and white striped paper bags. Glancing inside, Otterlie could see they had each been given a delicious looking stick of Welsh rock. Louise looked at her brother but as he was occupied, she managed to sneak it into her school bag unnoticed. 'Thanks, Hols,' they chorused.

'You alright?' Otterlie asked Arasuli shyly as they walked towards the Summer Class line up point. The struggle to articulate in English what he wanted to say was evident on his face but he managed to convey his exciting news to the three girls and Bertie who had turned to hear the update. 'Lady social worker found oumi, Oumi! We live in new room with Amir, Aam. We will get place to live soon. I am happy. So happy.'

'Your mum?' Louise queried. 'You found your mum?' As Arasuli nodded he was almost knocked backwards as the trio embraced him into a group hug. Bertie stood slightly to the outside of the group, obviously aware of the momentous implications but not sure whether to join in the celebration. Holly solved the problem by breaking free from the huddle to draw him in. All five children shrieked and jumped up and down until they were silenced by the whistle, signalling it was time to line up for the start of the school day.

Later that morning, after Mrs Redleigh had announced that Maths would go on for an extra quarter of an hour due to a special assembly being planned, Otterlie zoned out. The page of shapes and angles began to blur as her eyes suddenly prickled with the burn of impending tears. A sudden thought had hit her in the stomach; her mum wasn't coming back like Arasuli's! Before the plop of the first tear had reached her protractor, Mr George was by her side. He handed her a tissue and chivvied her out into the corridor. Both him and Mrs Redleigh had been prepped that morning that there might be some fragile souls in the classroom.

After her chat with Mr George, Otterlie felt a lot better. They'd drawn pictures together of her family and talked about how it was good that her and Elliot seemed to be getting on better at home. Her mind wandered thinking about this during assembly. She did not register the crucially important message about internet safety that was being taught to them.

When the bell rang for lunch and the girls joined the line to file outside, Otterlie shyly showed the drawing to her friends. Louise gave it a dismissive glance but slung her arm around

Otterlie's shoulders and led her friends towards the trees at the edge of the playground. They had netball practice in the afternoon so had tactics to discuss.

The fierce game that afternoon was refreshingly distracting. Summer Class had won against the slightly older children in Blossom Class and although it had been a friendly match, the mood was still jubilant as they hi-fived each other and cheered. Mrs Redleigh looked sweaty too and even though it had been an emotionally exhausting start to the week, she was still proud of her class. When they got back to the class, Mr George handed Otterlie the bib showing she'd be playing Centre and representing Mimosa in the county matches. Holly was to be Wing Defence but much to Louise's disgust she had been selected for the B team as the majority of the rest of the chosen A team were from Year Six. This worried Otterlie. She hated that Louise had been left out and she knew it could cause a bit of a problem in their friendship trio. The thunderous look on Louise's face said it all.

When the bell rang to signal the end of the day, Louise proved her point by ignoring Otterlie and Holly and hanging back to link arms with Allison. Otterlie cringed inwardly. She knew Louise was hurt and would punish them by not being their friend for a few days. In the past this had led to lots of unkind comments and tears. It wasn't like it was her fault though, they hadn't done anything wrong! Seeing Holly roll her eyes made her smile and the two of them headed out into the autumnal air. There was a police car parked just outside the gates, with two officers inside, but more interestingly there was a woman in a headscarf with unchecked tears streaming down her face beckoning towards Arasuli and wailing his name. 'Look, Hols, he really has found his mum!' They watched Arasuli allow himself to be drawn into a loving emotional hug. He didn't seem embarrassed by the commotion at all. He was beaming.

Laura and Poppy had watched the scene too. The fact that something so good had grown from something so horrendous proved that life wasn't all doom and gloom. Before Otterlie went past them to where Aimee was waiting, Laura stopped her and pressed a box of chocolates into her hands. 'Just a small something to say thank you for looking after Rufus and Shady last week,' she said gratefully.

'Thank you,' Otterlie responded politely and, grinning at Holly, she skipped off towards her stepmum, most of the stress from the day forgotten.

On Thursday evening Holly came out of school with Otterlie. A rare occurrence for a school night but Holly was going to sleep over. The girls had heard the adults discussing it the day before so had spent the day planning what fun they would get up to. Otterlie knew that Holly's mum had to take Poppy into the city for her court appointed counselling session and it might go on until late. Aimee had asked her not to mention it too much to Holly though because she got upset thinking about her sister being sad.

Before the girls got to the car there was a shriek as Bertie tripped and fell in his haste to avoid confrontation with some of the Year Six boys who were often mean to him. As Otterlie bent down to help him up she was almost knocked over by Louise who had rushed to her brother's aid. 'Leave my brother alone, just go off with Hippo Holly and don't interfere with my family.' Seeing Holly's skin pale and the tears spring to her friend's eyes made the rage flare in Otterlie's heart. How dare Louise talk like that, she was supposed to be their friend! True, Louise had been icy all week, but personal insults were a step too far.

Before she could control herself, she flung out her hand and grabbed a fistful of Louise's hair. 'What did you say?' Otterlie demanded.

Contempt flashed in Louise's eyes but then her face crumpled and she burst into tears. 'I'm so sorry, I didn't mean it. I... I... I'm just jealous...' Otterlie released her grip and, rubbing her head, Louise turned to look sheepishly at Holly. 'I really am sorry, I was trying to be nasty but I miss you both so much. Please will you be my friends again and forgive me?' Otterlie glanced at Holly who shrugged then pulled them all in together for a group hug.

Claudette and Aimee had watched the exchange with wary amusement but were both very pleased to see the girls reunited. Bertie's sudden agitation because he couldn't get into the locked car was enough to make the girls laugh as they helped him in with his bags. All the tension and angst evaporated. Some sort of secret adult code seemed to be going on and suddenly Louise was joining the other two in clambering into the back of Aimee's car. It was like they had never been apart and the shrieks and stage whispering from the back seat made Aimee smile as she drove all three girls back to her house for their dinner.

Feeling full of Aimee's delicious Spaghetti Bolognese, the girls were lounging contentedly in Otterlie's room discussing what colour to paint their toenails, when the door suddenly flew open and Elliot strode in looking at the phone in his hand. Without removing his eyes from the screen, he gestured and whispered, 'Ottie, I've done it, our secret! Like you wanted, I've found your mum on Facebook...' His voice trailed off as he looked at the three young faces staring at him. 'Oh, little people... there's loads of you. Um, I'll come back later. Shit.'

Muttering to himself he turned and left the room. For a few seconds the girls looked at each other in silence then the sound of Elliot's bedroom door slamming shut jolted Otterlie into action and she ran to question her stepbrother further.

Louise and Holly began frantically whispering, trying to speculate on what was going on but before they could discuss it in great depth, Aimee called up the stairs to let Louise know that her mum was there to collect her. Holly was the only one to wave Louise off and when questioned as to why Otterlie hadn't come down to say goodbye, Holly was perceptive enough to know that she couldn't divulge the little she knew so instead she lied and said Otterlie was in the toilet.

Chapter 14

Otterlie didn't say much to Holly when she returned to her room. She subconsciously righted the abandoned bottle of nail varnish then sat on her bed, hugging her knees, overwhelmed with new knowledge. Holly looked uncomfortable, as if she wasn't sure what to say to her friend. Without much communication but with no trace of an unfriendly atmosphere, both girls slowly got into their PJs and then took it in turns to brush their teeth in the bathroom before they climbed top and tail into Otterlie's bed.

If Aimee was surprised that they had gone to bed without a fuss on a school night sleepover she didn't comment when she went in to say goodnight. She hugged her stepdaughter, seemingly unaware that there was any problem, ruffled Holly's hair then wished them pleasant dreams and left them to it. She even ignored the fact the blow-up bed was unused on the floor but neither girl was perceptive enough to pick up on her absent-mindedness.

Under the comfort and protection of darkness Otterlie confided in her friend. 'Elliot said I shouldn't tell you, Hols, but he's done it. He actually found my mum on Facebook! She's changed her name but the picture of her playing netball is there on her page. There's baby pictures too but Elliot says it's not me, that she must have had another child which means I'm a big sister, I think.'

Holly reached for her friend's hand. 'Are you going to message her?' she asked sleepily.

There were a few moments pause before Otterlie replied, 'Yeah...' Before she elaborated the girls were interrupted by raised voices from downstairs. Jonny and Aimee were arguing, and it sounded serious.

The ruckus prevented them from falling asleep straight away, so they lay together in the dark room listening to the snippets of the heated adult conversation that carried up the stairs. It seemed to involve the ownership of the house, lack of money and something to do with Elliot and his school. Emotionally exhausted, Otterlie eventually drifted off to sleep, oblivious of the fact that Holly lay awake listening to information that didn't concern her.

It was Jonny who woke the girls for breakfast the next morning. He looked flustered and stressed but when questioned by his daughter as to where Aimee was, he just replied that she and Elliot had gone to visit Elliot's grandma. 'Why though, Dad?' Otterlie persisted.

Jonny didn't answer at first but then muttered, '...To cool off I guess.' He looked defeated as he left the room to get ready for work. Otterlie felt slightly concerned as she half-heartedly put out the breakfast things like she had watched Aimee do so many times. The argument must have been very bad. Aimee and her dad had never fallen out before. They were normally so cuddly and loving to each other. She mentioned this to Holly, who looked really tired and on the edge of tears herself, but Holly just shrugged and ate her Coco Pops. It seemed strange to leave the dirty breakfast stuff on the draining board in the kitchen but Jonny seemed not to give it a second thought as he hurried the girls into his work van. Otterlie glanced in the hall mirror as she was ushered past. It looked like both her and Holly were going to school with untamed hair. What else could possibly go wrong with their day? It was only eight a.m.!

The day did get worse. During break, Louise and Holly went off together leaving Otterlie on her own. She heard Holly tell Louise that it had been boring after Louise had gone home the night before.

Thinking about it, Otterlie realised it was probably true but it still hurt to hear it said aloud. Instead of following them she just sat on the bench by the Year Two playground. It had been decorated with hearts and stick people playing football and was named "The friendship seat" with the idea that if you saw someone alone on it you should go and ask them to play. Glancing around though, it didn't seem anyone had even noticed the significance of her sitting there. Laying down and putting her feet up on the back rest she sighed and thought about what Elliot had shown her on his computer. Her mum lived in another country, in what looked like a big house surrounded by palm trees and blue sky. Comparing it to the grey, dreary, November sky above her, she tried to imagine what it would be like to go there. Would her dad go too? Aimee wouldn't want to but she had made her dad sad this morning so maybe she would stay at home with Elliot, which might not be so bad, in case he started being horrible again. She suddenly remembered the other secret Elliot had told her. He was gay. She knew that meant he just fancied other boys not girls but for some reason she wasn't allowed to tell anyone that either. Keeping secrets was exhausting!

Otterlie played with Ewan and Harry at lunch break. They always thought she was great and with their encouragement she entertained them with rude raps and dance moves. Ewan was getting better at impersonating Eminem and could nearly keep up with her in the chorus. She allowed herself small glances to where Holly and Louise were huddled with Bertie and Arasuli but she was determined they would not know that they were crushing her heart.

The afternoon art project of creating dioramas of a scene in the rainforest was pleasantly distracting for the majority of Summer Class. Working in boy/girl partners, pre-decided by Mrs Redleigh, meant that complex friendship issues couldn't escalate further and shaping leaves and animals from the resources was therapeutic for the troubled young minds. Mr George commented loudly to Mrs Redleigh that he could almost see the blanket of calm descend on the class.

At the end of the day, it was her dad who was waiting by the gate. Jonny waved briefly at Laura and Claudette but it seemed to Otterlie that he deliberately avoided having to make conversation. She was glad. There was no way she'd have wanted to have to stand with Holly and Louise while the adults chatted anyway! Aimee wasn't mentioned. Instead, he drove back to work to finish a big repair job on a truck whilst Otterlie sat, subdued and tired, passing him tools until it was time to go home.

Thank goodness it was the weekend!

Chapter 15

The next few weeks felt a bit surreal in the Oapie household. Jonny kept picking up his phone, looking at it then sighing and putting it back in his pocket. Otterlie was also withdrawn. She was missing Aimee and, even though she wouldn't have thought it a few months earlier, Elliot's absence felt like a loss too. After school each day, Otterlie would go to her dad's garage and help pass him tools while he worked on fixing cars and vans. She had to admit the smell of the engines was comforting and she was learning quite a lot about mechanics too. The good thing about this new knowledge was that it impressed her current best friends. Louise seemed to have taken Holly away from her and although they weren't mean to each other, the friendship group seemed to have changed and alliances shifted.

Surprisingly though, Otterlie hadn't overthought this too much and instead she seemed to naturally gravitate towards playing with Ewan and Ruby during play time. Mrs Redleigh had decided to keep up her rotational system for the class seating plan which meant that usually, tight-knit friendships were separated during core lessons, which she said made them all have better concentration and fewer distractions.

Although Otterlie's day to day life had changed, it did not stop her thinking about what Elliot had shown her online about her mum. Most nights she lay awake thinking about what it would be like to see her. Would they look alike? Would they all live together? Would she be as good at making cakes as Aimee?

If only Elliot was around to help her research further.

On the fifth of December Jonny finally remembered to buy his daughter an advent calendar. It was a Thursday, so that afternoon, he made a special effort to get his day's work finished before collecting Otterlie from school. He knew he had a big job coming in on a Transit fleet the next day, meaning he would be working most of the weekend. When they got home, the two of them sat chatting in the kitchen while Jonny looked in the freezer to decide what they should have for dinner. 'Pizza or chicken nuggets or spag bol?' he asked.

Otterlie had been happily popping out her five accumulated advent chocolates but she paused to look hard at her dad. 'I miss Aimee. Please just call her, please, Dad. I want to see her and Elliot!'

She froze after she spoke, worried in case her dad got upset or even angry but instead he shut the freezer door, stood up, stretched, then sighed. 'You're right, Leelee Love, I will!' He pulled his phone from his pocket, ruffled her on the head and walked out of the room, into the garden, sliding the patio doors closed behind him.

Otterlie could see him chatting on the phone as he paced up and down the garden. She watched for a bit but lost interest when he sat himself on the bench outside Aimee's empty studio, his back to her. Putting the ingredients for Spaghetti Bolognese on the counter as a hint to her dad, she wandered up to her bedroom.

When her dad eventually called her down for dinner, Otterlie could see he was red-eyed but smiling. As he pushed a steaming bowl of spaghetti towards her, he nodded towards the garlic bread he had cooked from frozen. 'Can you tear that up for us please, LeeLee?' As she did as asked, he sighed then answered the unspoken query in her eyes, 'Aimee is going to come round on

Saturday. She needs to work in the morning in her studio anyway then she wants to spend the afternoon with you while I'm at work. Elliot will look after you as normal in the morning. Is that okay?'

Otterlie was empathetically old enough to know that this information wasn't actually the good news her dad had hoped for of a reconciliation between him and his wife, but it was a step closer to life feeling normal for her and she was grateful for that. Wordlessly, she shrugged and nodded but inside she was smiling and happy.

A pattern formed for the last few weeks of term. School consisted of all the usual Christmas activities, singing, carol concerts and watching seasonal films (although Otterlie was often envious of Ewan who got to go and bake cakes with the office staff whilst these were going on.)

At the weekends, Otterlie would spend Saturday with Elliot and Aimee as well as after school on Tuesdays, Wednesdays and Thursdays and the rest of the time it was just her and dad. Life wasn't perfect but it bumbled along.

That was until, after tricking her stepbrother into giving her extra information, Otterlie downloaded a train app and after planning her route to the airport, decided to use her savings from her moneybox to fly out to St Lucia for Christmas, to surprise her mum.

Chapter 16

Bertie

I was dreaming that I was falling and it woke me up. I was hopeful that I had been asleep for enough hours so that I would not be tired during my day. The room looked reassuringly familiar when I forcefully told my eyes it was time to open. As I reached out to turn on my radio, I could hear the echo of Louise's voice in my head telling me that I was a weirdo but I continued with my morning routine of listening to the world news. It grounded me. That's what Mum said, but I just like the sound of the reporter's voice floating around my room. Some people had got ill over the last month or so in a place in China and now nobody was allowed to travel there on holiday. I would look it up in my atlas later. Glancing at the school uniform in a neat pile on my chair, I decided it was time to get dressed. The shirt is the wrong one though, it's itchy and I know it will hurt my neck. Maybe today is not going to be a good day as I can feel the worry creep under my skin and make me feel hot and bothered.

Bertie kept his Spiderman pyjama top on but changed into the rest of his school uniform, taking care to make sure the seam of his socks was in perfect alignment with his toes. He wandered downstairs without turning on the light and went to stand under his favourite plant in the long hallway.

Stretching up on to his toes he inhaled the aroma of the

leaves while stroking the stem rhythmically with his fingers. Absorbed in his task, he jumped when his dad's voice startled him, 'Bertie, what on earth are you doing up? It's five-fifteen a.m.!' Stephen looked bleary eyed and was wrapped in his faded but much-loved dressing gown which had become a bit of a joke in their family. Bertie knew that his mum kept offering to buy him a new one but his dad always refused, saying that there was nothing wrong with the one he had. He could relate to this. Looking at his dad now he could tell that he felt warm and snuggly. Stephen sighed and yawned, turning towards the kitchen to put the kettle on.

Bertie followed.

The two of them sat in companionable silence, munching on their toast, Stephen engrossed in catching up on work emails and Bertie simply happy in his dad's company. When Claudette arrived in the kitchen an hour later, freshly showered and smartly dressed, she noted her son's strange attire but said nothing as she went through to the laundry room to find a different, clean and comfortable school shirt.

Experience had taught them all that some battles were not worth starting. She returned and helped Bertie into his uniform. He could sense that something felt different about today and it was making him feel anxious but then Louise appeared in the kitchen, clattering dirty water bottles into the sink, breaking the calmness of the morning. She was not in uniform and that reminded Bertie why today was different; Louise, Holly, Otterlie and Arasuli had to go somewhere special to make videos about what they had seen when the bad men had hurt Poppy. He had heard the adults have lots of conversations about it. He was worried about school though. Without all of them there, he would be at the mercy of some of the Year Six boys who called him names. His hand began to flap and he rocked his chair backwards and forwards, trying to comfort his trepidation.

'Relax, Bertiebum, today's not even about you. Stop being so dramatic.' snapped Louise, aggressively to her twin.

She flicked back her long, blonde hair and helped herself to a bowl of mixed fruit and muesli.

Bertie tried to relax but he couldn't control the feeling that something felt off. Lots of things had happened over the last few months, involving his friends and family, things that weren't normal and he didn't like the unsettling changes to his routine.

Stephen had to take Bertie to school that morning as Louise would be going off with her mum to meet the others before they had to go through their witness statements. This in itself was unusual, especially as Bertie was having to be dropped early at the newly set up breakfast club, run by Mr George. He and Louise had not been before but Bertie knew some of the others in his class had used the provision. As he climbed into his dad's sleek company car, Bertie thought about what had been happening since before Christmas.

Firstly, there had been the drama with Otterlie running away. She'd thought she could look for her mum and had managed to get herself to Gatwick Airport on the train. Bertie remembered the panicked tone in everyone's voices and the endless phone calls trying to locate her. Elliot had eventually confessed to searching online for Otterlie's mum, Ebony. The chaos had escalated until Jonny had received a phone call from the British Transport Police, informing him that security officials at the airport had found the young girl hiding by the British Airways check in desk.

Apparently, she had tried to buy a plane ticket. However, the airline was not in the habit of allowing nine-year-olds to make this transaction unaccompanied, nor would they have been able to get her very far with the £38.40 she had offered them for her fare. The whole thing had meant that Aimee and Jonny realised they loved and needed each other and they had all moved back in together so from what he'd overheard, Bertie personally thought that it had all turned out okay for Otterlie. Aimee was her new mum so she didn't need to worry about the other one she had who was called Ebony, who apparently did not want to be found anyway!

A few weeks after the drama, at a large New Year's Eve party hosted at his house, while the adults had all been drinking and dancing downstairs, Bertie had let Elliot play on his Xbox and Elliot had shown him new cheats on the game. He had thought Elliot was kind. They were friends now anyway; Elliot had promised him.

Stephen pulled up at the school gates then, breaking Bertie's train of thought. Seeing his dad glance worriedly at his watch, he tried to get himself out of the car quickly but as the playground was empty from its usual hustle and bustle. It felt wrong and Bertie found his feet wouldn't move. Instead they began to jig up and down. Even the under-breath swearing and the force of his dad slamming the car door as he marched towards the hall where breakfast club was located couldn't make Bertie's legs work. It was only seven forty-five in the morning but nothing was happening in the right order.

Mrs Rose appeared next to Stephen. Between them they cajoled and coaxed Bertie from the back of the car. He felt his hair being ruffled and a hurried kiss was placed on his cheek. The noise of his dad driving away caused the humming in his head to begin. It grew louder and louder. Yanking his arm away from Mrs Rose, he placed his hands over his ears, sank to the floor and began to moan and rock.

The calming, familiar voice of Mr George penetrated reassuringly through Bertie's fug. The overwhelming humming began to reside and Bertie allowed his TA to pull him to his feet and lead him into the hall. There was a table set up at one end with boxes of cereal, jugs of milk and bowls stacked precariously in a teetering pile as if they had been left there in a hurry, which indeed they had. Mrs Rose was holding the fort, ushering in a few children from various year groups and settling them with colouring and construction activities. Mr George knew that Bertie wasn't ready to join the other children yet so he steered him over to an area near the food table and settled him on a bean bag. 'Wait here, Mr Housten,' he commanded as he saluted to Mrs Rose and disappeared from the hall. Before Bertie had time to protest, he reappeared holding an iPad and some ear defenders. He was experienced enough to know that Bertie would be tired after his meltdown and would need time to recoup his emotions. Tapping the screen a few times, he then handed the device to Bertie. 'Complete a few rounds of this and then, when you are ready, Ducky, come help me with the breakfast.' Mr George bent down and placed the ear defenders over Bertie's ears, then he patted him on the shoulder and went and turned on the large screen for the other children. As the catchy theme tune for *Newsround* filled the room, Mr George tap danced over to Mrs Rose and thanked her for standing in.

She looked at him then spoke quietly, almost out of the children's earshot, 'Tom, you are a natural educator. I would be honoured if you would let me look into a funded route for you to pursue your teacher training, preferably through Mimosa so we don't lose you from our team.' He looked at her incredulously for a few moments then pulled the older woman into a hug. 'I will take that as your acceptance of my proposal,' she said with a smile and left him to run the breakfast club he had set up himself, to both boost his income and to offer grateful working parents a much needed service.

The monotonous block stacking game had relaxed Bertie and he stood up, removing the noise-cancelling ear defenders. As he wandered over to help Mr George as requested, his attention was caught by the news story on the large screen. The virus was spreading and there was concern it would spread all around the world. He tried the name out in his head, Covid-19.

Mrs Redleigh appeared at the hall door to gather up the KS2 children and send them to their respective classrooms to start the school day. Bertie trotted behind her, subdued. He was still uneasy about his routine being disturbed but the familiar smell of his teacher's musky perfume was a comfort. The other children in Summer Class filed in from the playground, bustling and shoving. After hanging up their coats and bags, everyone settled down to try the Maths morning activity on recapping adding fractions, which was ready for them on the board.

As it was Wednesday, it was singing assembly day. Mr George was leading it again this week. At the request of the other staff in the school, his natural ability to perform and make all the children feel included in the singing had meant it became his unofficial job role. Not that it looked like he minded, he embraced it with gusto every time!

Lunchtime was stressful for Bertie that day. The absence of his twin and the other missing members of Summer Class meant that he found himself alone on the playground. As he stood against the flint wall of the old building, he eyed the Year Six boys warily as they seemed to be making a beeline towards him.

'On your own today, Bert?' taunted Leighton whilst he looked back towards his friends for support. The other four boys jostled and shuffled forward so Bertie was trapped in a semi-circle with his back to the wall. 'What you gonna do, eh? Throw some chairs at us?' Bertie closed his eyes tightly, ignoring the jeering comments he could hear about him having a nap and falling asleep standing up. He thought about what his dad had said to him in the past about learning to calmly stand up for himself and he tried to focus on his breathing – he really did, but his foot flicked backwards and began a rhythmic tapping against the wall. He tried to zone out. The verbal assault from the boys had almost become white noise but the overwhelming whooshing feeling sweeping through his body and out of his ears had turned into rage. With an anguished howl he pushed off from the wall and ran blindly headfirst through the boys, sending two of them flying onto the unyielding playground surface. The momentum caused him to stumble but opening his eyes to focus, he managed to keep his balance and he ran in through the school entrance towards the relative safety of the upper Key Stage Two toilets. He sank onto the floor and hugging his knees tightly to his chest he began to rock backwards and forwards.

Mrs Redleigh found him curled up asleep under the sinks. His absence back to class after lunch had resulted in a small-scale search party, especially as the first-aider on duty had reported overhearing muttered comments from a couple of sheepish looking Year Six boys with grazed knees, palms and elbows. Gently shaking him awake, the sympathetic teacher pulled him to his feet, encouraged him to wash his hands and then led him towards Summer Class. She knew him well enough to be confident that he would not want a fuss, routine was the best thing to help calm him. The rest of the class were silently reading and barely registered the late arrival of their classmate. Mrs Redleigh settled Bertie in his chair, handed him his reading book and his water bottle and left him to it. She would chat with him casually during the afternoon when he was comfortable again and ready to talk.

Bertie frowned when he realised it was his dad by the gate at the end of the day. It wasn't that he didn't want to see his father, he did, but it was usually Mum on Wednesdays. Mrs Redleigh had been called into an urgent safe-guarding meeting as soon as the school day finished so it was Mr George who was over-seeing pick up. Stephen looked up as the TA escorted his son across the playground. It had not been the smoothest drop off that morning and judging by Bertie's sullen face the day obviously had not been great either.

Mr George told Bertie to have a good evening but was only rewarded by a monosyllabic response. Before Stephen could chastise him, Bertie had slunk into the backseat of the car and put his headphones on. 'I'm sorry about his manners…' began Stephen.

But before he could continue Mr George interrupted, 'Oh not to worry, Mr Housten, Poor Bertie has had a bit of an unsettled day today. The little lamb found himself overwhelmed several times and there was also an incident at lunchtime, dealt with of course, not to worry though,' he reassured. 'I will be keeping a very close eye on playground antics tomorrow, although with Louise and the others back I'm sure there won't be the same issues. I hope they all got on okay with the Crown Prosecution Service, poor duckies.' Stephen nodded in response but didn't need to reply as Mr George was called to deal with an issue over a lost lunchbox.

Chapter 17

Bertie had no further trouble with the boys in the year above over the next few weeks. Mrs Redleigh had provided a "calm box" for him during breaktimes and he'd been delighted to find his friend Arasuli turned out to be a strong competitor for him in Chess. When he had first pulled the chess set out of the box, Bertie had been worried nobody would play with him but Arasuli's face had lit up and the boys had strengthened their friendship further by becoming consumed in the game at every available opportunity. Mrs Redleigh began to feel concerned that the boys were isolating themselves from their peers but she didn't yet have the heart to suggest leaving the chess set alone as both her and Mr George could see the benefits for both boys.

Bertie proved to be a very good listener for Arasuli. He rarely interrupted or offered an opinion, instead just absorbed the flow of words, mainly in English but sometimes Syrian, that floated his way while they played their intense, strategic games. Arasuli's social worker had been into Mimosa Primary for several TAF (Team Around Family) meetings and all of the adults supporting the refugee family agreed it was good for Arasuli to share his story and they encouraged the conversations. Arasuli, his mum and uncle had also been learning English in special classes provided for them at the village hall.

The story Arasuli described sounded surreal to Bertie. It was so polar opposite from the comfortable, safe and privileged lifestyle that Bertie knew. However, his dad had helped him understand that everyone had different experiences of their journey through life and now he was kind of in awe of the literal journey that Arasuli had been on before he arrived at Mimosa Primary.

He learnt of how his friend had lived in a city that became unsafe, in a house with Yousef, his dentist father, his mother, Yara (who was very clever and always teaching him from their large library of books but she was not allowed to work outside the home), his Uncle Amir, Aunt Rima and Arasuli's grandparents had lived with them too. Arasuli described to his friend that his dad had decided they should flee to safety, but although his grandparents had sold their jewellery to help fund the trip, they had decided to stay in the Syrian city they had always lived in. It had been an emotional goodbye but sadly not uncommon amongst families desperate for survival. Bertie had thought of his own grandparents, whom he and Louise saw regularly; it would be horrible to leave them in a dangerous city and move away to a strange country with the rest of his family.

As he listened to the recount of walking across rough terrain for days and days, often while hungry, dirty and tired, Bertie looked down at the chess board. Some of the pieces seemed to be swimming a bit and he realised it was because his eyes had filled with tears. Wiping them away, he reached out his leg and gently nudged Arasuli. Understanding that Bertie was trying in his own way to show compassion, Arasuli grinned and punched him on the knee. 'Check!' he said proudly.

When he got home later that day, Bertie got his large atlas down from his book shelf. He loved maps. There was something comforting about seeing the world broken down into grids and sections. First, he looked up the place that was always featuring on the radio and in the news; Wuhan, China. He was fascinated with the variety of architecture there. His book of Chinese districts showed it to be a vibrant and busy place. He was so engrossed that Claudette gave up calling him down for dinner and had to climb the stairs to find him. He followed her down, clutching the heavy atlas close to his chest as they went into the dining room. While Louise chatted about her day, describing the various fallings out of other members of their class, Bertie opened the Atlas and spread it out next to his plate of risotto. He thought of all the information Arasuli had been telling him and, finding Aleppo, he traced his finger all the way through Turkey, over the sea to Greece, then from there to the South of England. It was a very long way!

As she got up to clear the plates, Claudette glanced at what Bertie was absorbed in. 'What you up to, Bert?' she asked.

'Look, Mum, this was Arasuli's journey!'

'That poor boy, what a tragic life he has had. That journey would have been enough to thwart any adult, let alone a small child.' Bertie looked solemnly into his mother's face as she said this.

'Oh, I know,' he told his mum. Stephen and Louise had paused their conversation and were listening too as he continued, repeating almost word for word what Arasuli had told him that day at school, 'His dad never made it onto the boat to England. Arasuli told me how his Auntie Rima, who was only fourteen, had gone missing when they were in the refugee camp in Greece. When they got there, there was no room in any tents so the whole family were forced to sleep on blankets with no shelter. He told me that he remembers looking around and all day hundreds of people would just be sitting. The children crying; the adults silent! Arasuli said it became normal. Anyway, late at night they would hear older teenage boys and young men trying to escape through the barbed wire fences to get into Europe. Some of them had made friends with his Uncle Amir but when he refused to go with them, they got angry. Amir knew people were being shot and beaten if they tried to escape so he did not want to go with them. One morning when they woke up, Rima was gone! Just vanished.'

Bertie paused and had a sip of his drink. He seemed oblivious to the impact his storytelling was having on his family. If he had looked up, he would have seen his sister leaning against their dad while he had his arms around her. Claudette had sunk back into a high-backed dining room chair and her eyes were bright with empathetic tears. 'So where did Rima go?' Louise asked, her voice came out quietly, not much louder than a whisper.

Bertie shrugged. 'They don't know! Amir thought that some of the mean men might have taken her when they were trying to escape because they were angry with him but Arasuli had heard his parents talking and they said something about girls being valuable.'

Claudette was no longer able to control the tears as they flowed down her cheeks but she was doing her best to not let her precious, innocent nine-year-old twins see the extent of her distress. She didn't dare catch Stephen's eye. She imagined he was struggling too. The world had so many dangers.

'So, Arasuli said that when they finally got offered the chance to get on another boat to England, his dad stayed in Greece to keep searching for Rima. Now both of them are lost!' Bertie did not appear distressed as he repeated Arasuli's tale. He did not feel emotionally connected, just pragmatic.

Stephen interrupted his son, who had stopped talking and

was repeatedly scraping his plate with his fork, 'You are a very good listener. What a good friend you are to poor Arasuli. Did he tell you how he got separated from his mother?'

'No, not yet. He's going to tell me about his boat journey next time we play Chess. I've finished my dinner so may I go back upstairs?'

Stephen nodded, so Bertie got up, taking great care to tuck in his chair. He gathered up his atlas and left the room.

Chapter 18

Bertie caught Louise's excitement as he came downstairs on Monday morning. It was the second of March which meant that it was Otterlie's birthday and, like they had done for Holly, they were giving her a kitten as a birthday present. Bertie knew it was all arranged and after school he would be meeting his mum at the school gates as normal but instead of going home, they were going to pick up the cat, then go round to Otterlie's house. His mum had told him that Elliot would be there too so Bertie was hoping he would be able to play on the computer.

Nothing overly exciting happened at school that day except for the fact there seemed to be a kind of unrest with the members of staff. Bertie caught snippets of whispered conversation, the word pandemic and references to Coronavirus and Covid-19 seemed to dominate but nothing was said to the children, so he didn't worry.

In Maths they had moved on from decimal numbers and were now learning how to convert improper fractions into mixed number fractions. Bertie found this soothing, he liked Mathematics. He knew where he stood with it – right or wrong and no grey areas. As he was finishing the questions, Mr George sauntered past his table, paused and glanced down at his work book. 'Nice job, Mr B Housten. Don't forget when you finish to go and get yourself the challenge sheet from the front.' Bertie knew this. Mr George knew that Bertie knew this. Every day though, Bertie would finish his Maths tasks, usually before everyone else, and then just sit and wait until he was reminded to get up and get the next sheet. As he looked up at his TA, Mr George flashed him a grin and performed his best muscle man pose. 'You've got this, Bertie!'

At the end of the day, Louise, Otterlie and Holly rushed out into the playground in front of Bertie. He hung behind, by the pegs, unrushed and carefully zipped his lunch box into his rucksack. Harry Year from his class was still by the coats too, holding one shin pad and rummaging in his bag, probably looking for the other! Neither boy spoke. Once his bag was organised how he liked it, Bertie sauntered out to the waiting group. Across the road, Arasuli and his mum were waving at him. Somewhat self-consciously, he waved back then climbed into the backseat of his mum's car and put his headphones on. His dad had made him a playlist of calming music on an old iPod and it always relaxed him during the daily transition from school life to home life.

They pulled up outside Claudette's friend's house and she jumped out, leaving the twins in the car. Louise was fidgeting with excitement at the thought of taking the new kitten to Otterlie's house but Bertie was indifferent to the situation and stayed absorbed in his world of violin concertos. In only a few minutes, Claudette was back with a pet carrier in her arms and flashes of white fur could be seen through the slits in the side. Depositing it gently on Louise's lap, they set off for the estate where Otterlie lived, which was on the other side of the village.

Bertie felt extremely overwhelmed as his mum coaxed him out of the car and into the Oapie's house. He could hear his sister, Otterlie and Holly cooing and squealing with adoration in the front room where they had run to meet the new snowy kitten. They would not want him interrupting them though. Poppy was curled up on the kitchen sofa with her eyes closed and her ear pods in.

Bertie was a bit scared of her. He'd heard adults talking conspiringly over the last few months, saying things like; how she was coping so well considering, she was fragile, incredibly brave, withdrawing into herself, amongst other sentiments. He stared at her. She looked just the same to him, she was just Holly's big, moody sister!

He trailed behind his mum as she walked through the kitchen and into the back garden, where Jonny had turned on the patio heater and was now busying himself firing up the BBQ. Aimee was talking to Laura and the two woman looked up as Claudette approached. They beckoned her over to the empty chair next to them. 'How are you, Bertie?' asked Aimee. 'Would you like a drink? There's plenty to choose from on the side in the kitchen, please help yourself.' The anxious feeling began in Bertie's stomach and crept upwards towards his throat. He knew Otterlie's stepmum but suddenly he couldn't articulate his words to answer her. His foot tried to compensate by tapping itself on the patio slabs but his hands joined in and became agitated too. He focused his eyes to the ground. This wasn't a normal Monday afternoon. They should be at home. Not here.

'Hey Mate, wanna play some Minecraft?' Elliot's voice penetrated through Bertie's fug. He looked up, the panic in his throat subsiding back to his stomach, then evaporating completely. Elliot had called him his mate! He had meant what he said before about them being friends! Nodding and grinning he followed Elliot back into the house and upstairs without a backwards glance at his mother or the other adults.

When Jonny called into the house to let everyone know the food was ready, they all trooped outside to fill their plates with the delicious smelling delights that he had cooked. Although it was early March it wasn't overly cold and the outside heater kept off any chill. The girls ate quickly and were soon begging to go back inside to continue playing with newly named Daisy, the kitten. Aimee insisted they sing to Otterlie all together first though and they had just launched into "Happy Birthday" when Stephen arrived, fresh from work and still in his smart business suit. Bertie observed his dad take the proffered beer, nod his thanks and join straight in with the remainder of the song. Once the girls had made their escape, to Otterlie's room this time, Elliot and Poppy decided to go and watch TV together in the front room. Bertie shook his head at Poppy's offer of joining them and instead he sat in the swing chair by Aimee's studio and let the adult conversation, from the patio, wash over him.

Jonny had asked Stephen about the new virus. From what Bertie could understand it seemed to be spreading around the world and his dad was telling the others that he'd had a few overseas trips cancelled or postponed. Bertie thought the virus might be a good thing if it meant his dad was at home more often! Laura said that the local GP had recommended to her to take supplements of vitamins when she had had to go in for a check-up last week. Aimee added that several of her hairdressing clients had also mentioned taking vitamins but to avoid anything containing Ibuprofen.

'It might come to nothing yet,' Claudette said.

'Hopefully,' Laura replied. 'We don't need anything else to hold up the dreaded court case!'

As the conversation changed to questions and murmured sympathy for Poppy and the awful things she had been through, the adults lowered their voices. Otterlie's luck at being found safe and sound was mentioned too but Bertie switched off. He had heard most of it before anyway. Using what information he had gathered from his eavesdropping, Bertie thought to himself about the virus that was coming. He had researched more about China recently and it all seemed a bit strange to him that someone eating a bat, like he had heard in the news, could cause germs to spread around the world. All the way to England!

The daylight had practically vanished and Bertie was cold so he got off the swing chair and went towards the laughing group of adults. 'Can we go now?' he asked his dad. Stephen raised his eyebrows and looked sternly at his son. They had talked before about how words like that could be seen as rude if they were guests at someone else's house. Bertie didn't care though; he'd had enough and he was sure it was supposed to be bath time. He allowed his dad to pull him onto his lap and wrap him in a bear hug. It felt safe and warm. He would never let anyone else touch him like this though, not even his mum.

Chapter 19

The story of *Gangsta Granny* being acted out, in the school hall, by a few keen teachers, was just white noise to his ears. Much more pressingly, Bertie was itchy and uncomfortable. The fabric touching his arms was making the hairs feel funny and he pushed his sleeves up and rubbed his skin vigorously. It had felt okay at home before he left for school. Mum had checked with him several times but he had told her it was fine. His arms began to hurt with the intensity of the sensation and he let out an involuntary, distressed yelp. He was oblivious to the children around him who were nudging each other and whispering at him to be quiet. He jumped when a hand touched him on the shoulder but realising Mr George was leaning towards him across the row of other members of his class, he got up and let himself be led out of the school assembly.

When they got into the Summer Classroom, Bertie was surprised to see Arasuli sitting there. He had a sign round his neck, written in Mrs Redleigh's distinctive teacher handwriting, saying, 'I'm a Muggle!' Before greeting his friend, Bertie struggled out of his synthetic black dragon hoodie (with spikes and a tail added) and threw it to the floor. The static left his hair standing up for a few seconds. He hated dressing up and every year finding a costume for World Book Day was a chore. He knew his mum had thought it was safe this year to go simply dressed and he was wearing black joggies with a black t-shirt. The offending item had been a last-minute online purchase and had completed his "Toothless the Dragon" outfit. He was never putting it back on! Louise's outfit had been much more elaborate and he recalled her proudly twirling to show off her Violet Beauregarde masterpiece to her friends, as they had trooped into assembly.

Once free of the sensory nightmare, Bertie felt more relaxed and went and sat next to his friend. Mr George disappeared and then reappeared a few minutes later with a carton of milk and a banana for each boy. He put the chess set on the table and retreated to Mrs Redleigh's desk where the English Books were open and ready to be marked from the earlier literacy lesson. After the extended WBD celebratory assembly had finished, the rest of the class would go straight out to break so they would be undisturbed for a while.

Arasuli still hadn't spoken. He leaned across the table and grabbed a banana, peeling it hungrily. Bertie regarded his friend. He looked sad. Worse than sad. 'You all right?' he asked more gruffly than he wished. Arasuli shrugged but began setting up the white pieces on the board, pushing the black set towards Bertie. Companionably, Bertie mirrored the actions until the board was ready to play.

As the game commenced, Arasuli found his voice. 'Social worker thinks my dad dead. No records found of him. Oumi cry all time. No money for food, Amir sad too. Yuma say he need wife to make him happy.' A tear plopped onto the chess board but the second one was brushed away before it left Arasuli's chin. Bertie looked at the board. He used his knight to take a stray bishop before speaking.

'My mum works at the food bank; she will make sure you are not hungry any more. Shall we go outside? You are not playing this game well today; I'm winning too easily. My dad says fresh air is good for the soul!'

Mr George smiled sadly as he waved the boys out to play. These young people had to deal with such tough circumstances.

Outside on the playground, there was a feeling of over-excitement hanging in the air. There always was when it was not a normal uniform day. Arasuli had run straight to join in with an elaborate game of Stuck in the Mud which had been given a new twist by some of the Year Six children. From what Bertie could determine, if you were caught you had to pretend to be dying from Covid-19 until someone came along and rescued you. He shivered; the wind was cold on his bare arms but there was no way he wanted his dragon hoodie back on. He was hopping around, not wanting to join in the game, when he saw Holly and his sister over by the thinking tree. Bertie walked over and stood expectantly, waiting for them to acknowledge him.

It was Holly who greeted him. 'All right, Berts? You wanna play?' She gestured towards the noughts and crosses grid they had drawn in the mud with a stick. Louise rolled her eyes at the intrusion but said nothing as her brother plopped himself down onto the grass next to her. Her bright purple face paint had smudged a bit on her left cheek, but she didn't seem to care. Bertie wondered if he should tell her, but decided against it.

Holly handed him the stick and he drew a wonky cross in the centre space. He guessed he had interrupted their chat as they were unusually quiet so he attempted what his dad would call an ice-breaker. 'I like your costume. You look fierce!'

'Thanks,' Holly replied with a sudden grin, 'I'm Mrs Trunchball, I put annoying children in the Chokey!'

Before she could say anything else, a long shrill whistle made them jump. Bertie covered his ears but Holly and Louise pulled him to his feet to follow the playground rules. It wasn't the end of break but Mrs Rose had caught the group playing the "Covid game" and had stopped everyone on the Year Five and Six playground to explain why that was an inappropriate game and how it was in very bad taste in light of the situation spreading around the world. Louise covered her mouth with her hand and whispered to Holly, 'What's bad taste mean anyway? What is she on about?' Holly shrugged in response. They watched the headteacher disperse the group of children. Arasuli looked a bit forlorn and was shuffling around looking unsure where to go so Louise nudged Bertie. 'Go and see if he's all right,' she prompted.

Bertie didn't forget his promise to Arasuli when he got home that evening. He wandered into the kitchen to find his mum. She was singing quietly to love songs on the radio while stirring a wok full of steaming, delicious smelling, vegetarian chilli.

'Mum?' he began. Claudette looked at her son. It was unlike him to initiate a conversation like this, especially as he was frowning and looking pensive. 'You okay, Bertie? Can I help you with something?'

He looked up at his mum through his lowered eyebrows. 'We need to give Arasuli and his mum and uncle all the food at the food bank. He says he gets hungry and that's even though his uncle gives him some of his own food as they don't have enough. I told him you will sort it out! Can we take it to them?'

Claudette smiled sadly before she answered, 'You are really growing up to be a lovely young man, I'm proud of you. The food bank is complicated though, Bertie. It's not my food to give out and Arasuli's family will need to be referred but I will do what I can to get them in the system. Tonight though, shall we share our dinner?' On his nod, she opened the large cupboard above the built-in fridge and began to take out an assortment of plastic-lidded containers. Together they filled them with the bubbling chilli, salad, garlic bread and a selection of homemade chutneys. Bertie disappeared through the French doors, into the vast garden and then reappeared with a bunch of handpicked daffodils. Claudette grimaced at the thought of her meticulous flower beds being disturbed but she didn't comment. Smiling at her son, she took the proffered flowers, wrapped the stems in damp kitchen roll and added them with all the food into a large picnic hamper.

As soon as Stephen got home from work to look after Louise, Bertie and his mum packed the food into the car and set off to the outskirts of town where the temporary accommodation was situated.

Chapter 20

The news that Boris Johnson might consider putting the country into a lockdown was creating a hum of anxiety amongst most adults over the next week. Whispered speculation about what might happen seemed to be all the adults were discussing.

Stephen had thought it wouldn't really affect their family too much but then his boss from New York called him to say that they were grounding all staff and nobody in the company would be flying for business. The situation began to seem very real. The company he worked for relied on its staff circulating the world for meetings.

After lunch, Bertie and Louise were sent out to play in the treehouse. Although it was mid-March the air was quite warm and the weekend stretched in front of them excitingly.

Louise sighed, stretched and then looked at her brother. 'I heard Mum on the phone,' she said.

'Me too,' replied Bertie, 'I don't think we will be going to London for our new shoot next week!'

'Arrrrhhh it's not fair,' moaned Louise dramatically. 'The job was for an awesome, cool brand and they had said we could keep the clothes this time. I saw the contract. I was going to get extra t-shirts for Otterlie and Holly too.' She flung herself back on to the large, musty smelling bean bag and threw her hands above her head. Bertie wasn't sure how to respond. He rubbed the pads of his fingers together and stared at the wooded slats of the floor. He knew that it was because of the virus and Mum had said it was not a great time to travel into a city. She had been discussing with their agent on the phone about the fear of the unknown that was sweeping alarmingly across the world. People in other countries were dying and images on the news showed people encompassed in scary looking white suits. He remembered watching the film ET and it had reminded him of a scene from that.

He had also glanced at his mum's phone whilst she had been scrolling through Facebook. He had snuck into bed next to her early that morning, when his dad had been in the shower. Although he had pretended to not look at her personal account (he knew this was an invasion of privacy), he could not un-see the video of a scene, supposedly from a Chinese city, with people looking like they were being left to die on benches in the street. It all seemed very far-fetched and unimaginable.

Bertie's reverie was broken when Holly's voice called out to Louise from below. He stepped back to make room for her to scramble through the trapdoor then he descended quickly before they began their girl chats. He wandered back towards the patio and almost bumped into Otterlie who was rushing out to join the others in the garden. 'Hi, Berts, you okay? Your mum said you were all outside. You gonna hang out with us?'

Bertie shook his head in response to Otterlie's greeting and nodded towards the treehouse. 'They are up there…' He watched as she ran off, shouting thanks over her shoulder.

Laura, Aimee and Claudette were in the kitchen joking that it was five o'clock somewhere as they sat, perched on high stools, around the kitchen island. They were contemplating opening an expensive bottle of fizzy wine. Bertie stood uncertainly by the door not sure whether to enter. The ladies had hushed their voices but he could still hear the concerned tones of his mum asking

Laura if she could actually drink with her medication. Her reply was, 'Drinking keeps me sane, it's better than the other stuff!' The sound of the cork popping made Bertie jump and he knocked into the door frame.

Aimee appeared at his side, holding a flute of wine, 'Oh hi, Bertie, I thought you were Otterlie lurking there. Did she find your sister and Holly okay?' He nodded shyly and stayed in his position by the door even after Aimee had thanked him and gone back to join the others. He wasn't sure he liked all these people being in his kitchen. It smelled like too many mixes of strong perfume!

The laughing adults paused as Stephen came into the kitchen. He declined any of the proffered alcohol but stood chatting politely with his wife's friends for a few minutes before noticing Bertie, who was quietly rocking on the balls of his feet. 'Ah there you are, are you ready? We don't want to keep young Arasuli waiting, do we?' He put out his arm and gently touched Bertie on the shoulder, nudging him towards the majestic, leafy hallway. 'Go and get your shoes and jacket, Son. Good job we are getting all the play dates in this weekend, ladies. Who knows what it will be like next week if this shiz really hits the fan...' Laura looked worried but Aimee pulled her into a hug. Claudette grimaced at her husband. Mouthing a remorseful apology, he said his goodbyes and caught up with Bertie who was waiting patiently by the front doors.

When Claudette had taken the food to the Deeb family the previous week she had discovered them in a very run-down self-contained bedsit. The dingy access corridor through the old converted house had smelt strongly of a mixture of urine and sweet-smelling smoke and had been lit only by a flickering naked bulb. Bertie had shrunk next to her, clinging tightly to her arm.

However, Arasuli had opened the bedsit door with a bright, welcoming smile and had proudly led them into the room to where his hard-working mother, Yara, was balanced precariously on the rickety headboard, humming and washing the ceiling.

As she climbed down, Bertie had thrust the daffodils at her then stood back. The brave, young woman, who had been through so much, then did something unexpected. She had sung. It was a haunting sound, a beautiful tarab that made Claudette's hairs jump out of the goosebumps on her arms. Arasuli led Bertie to sit on the wooden, straight-backed chairs by the window and they all listened spellbound to the Syrian folksong. The abrupt banging on the plywood interior wall, followed by shouts of "Shut up that infernal racket" had broken the trance.

Yara had been ever so grateful and had insisted they all stay for a while. She had tried to offer Claudette money, scrambling round in her purse and sorting through the coins before admitting defeat to Claudette's protests and humbly said "thank you". The visit had ended with a promise of a trip to the park for the boys, which Arasuli had translated for his mother. According to Amir, who had arrived home from a long day at work just as they were leaving, Arasuli had been worried about having a day out without his mother, having only just been reconnected with her, but he knew she needed the break.

On hearing of the social arrangements, Stephen had volunteered to chaperone the boys' day out and he had escalated it from a few hours in the local playpark to an afternoon adventure. He and Bertie were now setting off to collect Arasuli for a trip into town to find the new trampoline park.

Bertie bent down and shifted the seam on his special socks. His dad had explained it was non-negotiable to wear them because they had special grips on the bottom, so he was trying his hardest to ignore the itch that was slowly creeping up his legs. He looked at Arasuli who was waiting patiently in the line to go into the trampoline area, his face full of amazement. Neither of them had been there before, each for their own personal reasons, but the excitement was so far outweighing the apprehension that fluttered in Bertie's stomach. As the gate opened, they surged forward with the other children and found themselves bouncing high towards the vast ceiling of the old, converted hangar. After a few minutes, Bertie knew he needed his noise-cancelling headphones. The laughs, shrieks and general volume of happy, energetic children were vibrating around the cavernous building and causing the anxiety to surge through his veins. Leaving Arasuli happily trying to flip himself over a padded side wall to land in a pit of foam, Bertie clambered back towards where his dad was sitting in the café, chatting with a couple of other parents. They were drinking coffee whilst their children played. Stephen saw him coming and instinctively reached down to retrieve the headphones from the bag that Claudette had packed before they left. 'Here you go, Bert, try these and go back and help Arasuli, I think he is queuing for the inflatable sumo suits. Remember the friends code we talked about in the car – you stay together and look after each other!' Bertie looked a bit uncertain as he glanced back towards his friend but he took a deep breath and repeated the mantra in his head. His dad had turned and continued his conversation with a lady who was rocking a small baby on her lap. They were talking about the pandemic again. Apparently there was going to be a lockdown soon. Whatever that was!

Chapter 21

Thomas George

I had woken up early again. It seemed to be happening more often than not lately but judging from the clattering noises and the aromatic smell of coffee and bacon which was drifting up the stairs, it appeared that Mum was up too. Or maybe she had just not gone to bed yet. My phone alarm hadn't gone off yet so it was before six a.m. My mum, Rachel, works shifts as a care home supervisor and she often finds it tricky to sleep as she keeps really irregular hours. She is more my best friend than my mother, especially as there are only sixteen years between us and she had raised me on her own. My dad had vanished when she was pregnant with me, leaving her alone after promising her the world. He reappeared through various stages of my childhood – always on the scrounge for money, to get himself out of the crippling debts he had racked up with his gambling addiction. Mum had always held firm and never given him a penny of her precious hard-earned cash. He did nothing to contribute towards my life or give my mum any kind of parental support in any way. Last time we had seen him was almost ten years ago. I'd been a hormonal thirteen-year-old and going through struggles at school because of my sexuality. He had called me an offensive homophobic name in response to me telling him to stop asking us to feed his addiction and Mum had reared her protective, maternal, peacock feathers and punched him square in the nose.

He had not graced us with his unwanted presence since. I was proud of her for it. She was a strong woman and we were a team. Just the two of us.

Dozing in bed, contemplating how much I love her, she suddenly appears at my bedroom door, knocking before she enters. Giving up on sleep, I gratefully take the tray she thrusts towards me and nod to her request to sit on the end of my large king-size bed, which takes up most of the bedroom. Blowing her a kiss, I tuck into the Full English breakfast she has prepared for me. 'Mum, you spoil me!'

She grins and looks about twenty years old, like the sister people mistake her for when they see us out together. Especially when she introduced herself affectionately as my fag hag when we were painting the town red last weekend! Her grin fades and a serious frown settles across her features.

'Have you been online yet this morning?' I shake my head as my mouth is full of sausage. 'Boris is saying that Friday will be the last day of school. They are all to close and everyone who can has to stay at home. From next Monday, the whole country will be in national lockdown because the death rate is so high with the virus spreading everywhere!' Staring at her, I scrabble under the tartan duvet for my phone and scroll frantically through the news stories from the last twenty-four hours. It is true. The Prime Minister has announced that all schools are to close at the end of the week until further notice. Although there are to be exceptions for key worker children.

I wonder what this means for me. Will I still be paid? According to the lists online, Mum is now to be classed as an essential key worker. Her job role suddenly seems significantly more dangerous and patriotic. She hugs me, then leaves me to my thoughts as she collects my breakfast remains and heads back downstairs. She really is an angel!

The sombre atmosphere was heavily lurking in the corridors as Thomas walked into work. He had fifteen minutes to acclimatise before going to set up the breakfast club. A few teachers were gathered around the photocopier in the primary office area, quietly speculating about what a national lockdown would entail. Mrs Rose looked incredibly stressed and emotional as she quietly responded to the good morning salutations from all the staff. 'Staff meeting at three-fifteen today, please spread the word…' Everyone nodded gravely in response as the headteacher went into her inner office and closed the door.

Thomas took a deep breath and pulling up his metaphorical big boy socks. He forced his trademark spring into his step and skipped down the corridor to find Mrs Redleigh. 'Morning, beautiful,' he chirped as he snuck up behind her in Summer Class, making her jump. Walking over to the classroom sink, he wet a paper towel and handed it to the teacher, indicating her navy shirt collar. 'I think baby Clara may have left you a little present from breakfast!' Sophia Redleigh rolled her eyes as she scrubbed furiously at the soggy Weetabix her youngest child must have rubbed kindly onto her work clothes, before she had been dropped at nursery.

'It was manic at the crèche door this morning, Thomas. I almost had to stamp my feet to get recognised as being a key worker ready for next week. They are going to run on a complicated points scheme from Monday, using a skeleton staff for only the most desperate key worker parents while the rest of the setting is closed like the schools. I need to speak to Mrs Rose to clarify what is going on but when I popped in this morning, she was on the phone to the council and she waved me out! Plus,

Ethan is only eleven. I know he is at secondary school now but I can't leave him home alone to fend for himself when his school shuts! Oh, and you know Luke won't step up, he's more worried Boris won't let him go and watch the Footie with his mates.' Finishing her outburst, Sophia visibly crumpled and promptly burst into tears.

Thomas wrapped her in his arms. 'It will all be right. Mrs Rose has called a meeting for after the children go home at the end of the day. Hopefully she will have all the answers we need.'

As professional as ever, Sophia was fully composed and smiling at the children as they entered the classroom three quarters of an hour later. Thomas had great respect for his colleague as she spent time after registration explaining to the children that the prime minister had declared Friday would be their last day at school for a while. She put *Newsround* on for those who had not been in breakfast club that morning and handed out some iPads so the children could do some research about the virus for themselves.

Thomas tried his best to liven the heavy, expectant atmosphere that shrouded the classroom. Eight children were absent, their parents fearful about the risk of staying in school until the end of the week. He looked at Mrs Redleigh and gave her the sign for an extra break in their secret code. She nodded and managed a smile. 'Come on then, me hearties, we are going outside for a game of Rounders. The fresh air will do us all the world of good and blow away these glum faces!' The children whooped and lined up behind Mr George. Walking like a crazy monkey, he led them out into the sunshine and began organising teams.

The children threw themselves into the game, whooping and cheering in encouragement of their team players. Thomas and

Sophia stood behind the backstop. Keeping one eye on the game, they could also sneak the chance for a quick catch up on a few members of the class without being overheard. Arasuli skidded across the grass, completing his rounder with a smile lighting up his usually serious features. Mrs Redleigh nodded towards him, 'He's a changed chap since he's been reunited with his mother. Amir was doing his best but he's only young himself and both those poor boys needed love and guidance from a parental figure.'

Mr George nodded and lowering his voice he whispered back, 'Oh I know, that poor woman though – losing her husband and extended family. It doesn't bear thinking about. How their family was torn apart and what they went through to find themselves somewhere safe to call home!' He broke off as Mrs Redleigh had spotted Holly's face dissolve into tears after she tumbled, rather ungraciously, over the second base marker. Once Holly's knee had been given the once over and order restored to the game, they continued their conversation. 'Did you hear Arasuli recount to Bertie what happened to his dad, Yousef? I went home and cried so much for them. It still makes the hairs stand up on my arms now when I think about it.' Sophia visibly shivered in the sunshine as she said this to Thomas.

'I know, poor loves, you can't imagine it, can you? Your fourteen-year-old auntie just vanishing. Then your dad too! All in a strange camp in a strange country. Arasuli was so matter of fact as he told his story to Bertie but I wonder if that was because of his concentration on speaking in English. I was so impressed with his description; you wouldn't know that it was less than a year ago that the poor lamb and his uncle found their way to the doors of Mimosa!'

Mrs Redleigh murmured her agreement then added her

contribution to their wonderment of Arasuli and the terrible things that had happened to his family. 'Oh, I agree, it's been so lovely to see Mrs Deeb reunited with her son and nephew. Her English comprehension is coming on too. Even over the last few weeks of her taking English lessons at the village hall. I hope they don't stop them with this lockdown business. Social services are still in contact with all sorts of organisations trying to trace her husband and niece. It seems that the opportunity to get onto a boat presented itself while they were at that awful camp in Greece. Yousef had persuaded his wife and the boys to get aboard. He'd even secured them all life jackets which had been a rare successful accomplishment. He then left, disappearing back towards the camp, saying he would follow when he had Rima. Their family case worker told me that in the chaos of boarding the boats, a riot had broken out with desperate people, who had no money left to pay for their passage, trying to get themselves aboard too. In the kerfuffle, Yara had been separated from the boys. Poor, dear Arasuli had watched his mother be roughly knocked into the water but before he or Amir could get to her, their boat had launched and the last they had seen of her was her scrambling urgently into another, vastly overcrowded, boat.'

'The brave boys had no idea if she was alive! Thankfully, her boat had landed safely too in the UK but way up north somewhere. She had been taken to a detention centre but desperately and determinedly pleaded her case and continued her quest to find her son and nephew. Through various channels and the amazing work of charities, she had been reunited when the boys' names came up in relation to Holly's sister's case. Every cloud and all that. Although that is a whole other horrendous story. The things these innocent children have to experience and be exposed to, it's just soul destroying.'

Nodding his agreement, Thomas gave Sophia a bittersweet grimace and nodded towards the Rounders game. One team seemed to be losing interest as their opponents kept catching them out. 'Shall we?' he asked. At her sudden grin, his own face lit up and after waiting for the teacher to kick off her heeled wedges, the two of them went to join in the game, one on each team with Sophia joining the line of waiting batters.

In true Mimosa style, to the chants of "Go, Mrs Redleigh, go…" she whacked the ball far across the field and ran to first base. Thomas saw that Ola wasn't going to catch the ball this time so he loudly joined in the chant, enthusiastically encouraging his own team too and soon the whole class was laughing and whooping as their teacher continued her run, skidding ungainly around the bases before collapsing with grass-stained trousers and feigned exhaustion onto the ground, having secured a morale boosting rounder for her team.

Chapter 22

The staff meeting reassured Thomas slightly. Headteacher, Georgina Rose, stood patriotically on the stage and talked about the recent announcement from the Government and the outcome of subsequent briefings from the local council. Encouraging a united sense of coming together to protect each other from the spreading virus, she promised that, as a school, they would try their best to support the community whilst keeping each other as safe as could be. She explained that the members of staff who had any pre-existing medical conditions or young children would be on the working from home rota – setting and monitoring home learning work for the children. The rest of the staff would be on an initial two weeks in school, two weeks working from home set up, with those in school to look after the key worker and vulnerable children. The list of who would be eligible was being rapidly worked on. Emails having already been sent out to parents to assess need.

Sophia remarked quietly to Thomas that she was sure Arasuli would be offered a place. He nodded, then whispered back, 'Yes, there might be several from our class. We have quite a few key worker parents too, Isla and Luna will qualify I'm sure, plus Ewan – isn't his mum a supermarket manager?'

They paused their discussion at a frown from Mrs Rose who then continued to outline how the new systems would work. Thomas mentally went through the class register. Callum, Joe and the Wullims twins had parents in the new key worker definition category. All four of them attended breakfast club as their parents went off on early shifts at the hospital.

A quick training session on how to use the online, home learning program would take place on Friday. The school was waiting for their I.T guy to finish setting it up but she had full hope it would be ready to go for the following Monday. Thomas thought despairingly of the ancient laptop he shared at home with his mum. Hopefully it would be powerful enough to be usable. He grimaced to himself. It would need to be dusted off and taken out of the ironing board cupboard!

To save himself the worry of technology issues straight away, he volunteered as soon as the harassed headteacher asked the question, to be on the team to come into school on the Monday – the first day of the national, historic lockdown. Looking around the large hall, he could see the worried, apprehensive faces of his colleagues. They were seated in key stage clusters around the room and the EYFS (Early Years Foundation Stage) team were whispering worriedly amongst themselves. The fear of the unknown was rife and mirrored in the teary, apprehensive eyes of everyone. Comforting though, was the fact that, as key workers themselves, they would all be on full pay. However, their role might change over the coming weeks. Thomas' mind wandered and he wondered what would happen to his second job. Surely supermarkets would be considered essential and stay open too?

The last Friday before national lockdown was a very surreal day. Thomas and Sophia grimly noted the absences of yet more members of their class. Families were getting wary of the risk of infection spreading and more had pulled their children out of school to keep them safe at home. They had just seventeen children answer the morning roll call. After a quick meeting with other Key Stage Two teachers, Mrs Redleigh announced to the expectant faces of her charges that they would be abandoning the lesson planning and instead having an easy day. Louise and Otterlie let out a whoop of delight and the mood in the room shifted to a more jubilant "end of term" type of energy.

Taking a deep breath, Thomas smiled at the children. 'Let's get this show on the road, Mrs R. Shall we let them SWTL?'

Louise's keen ears pricked up at the acronym. Although she threw her twin a slight glance of concern, knowing he did not like to move from his designated seat, she nudged Arasuli. 'Mr George is saying we should sit where we like. Will you go next to Bertie so he doesn't have to move?'

Sensing that there would be no issues, Mrs Redleigh gave the command, giving the children thirty seconds to switch seats to be closer to their friends, pretending she would change her mind if they were too slow. She then handed round large sheets of sugar paper, challenging the groups on each table to produce ideas of what they would like to do at home when there were no options to leave the house unnecessarily, for the foreseeable future.

Holly, Louise, Otterlie, Ewan, Arasuli and Bertie had bonded into a tightknit friendship group over the past few weeks and the six of them had rushed to work together on the same table. As Mr George wandered round the classroom, he was impressed by the activities they had written down or sketched. Otterlie had her concentration face on as she drew an elaborate obstacle course involving tunnels and wooden beams and Bertie was captioning a stickman version of himself rearranging his bookshelves.

He overheard a conversation between Holly and Louise which he made a mental note to flag to Mrs Redleigh at the end of the day. Apparently, Holly had heard her mum on the phone saying that due to the pandemic, her sister's upcoming court case preparation was being postponed. The men had pleaded not guilty so it was going to trial. Already, it seemed to be causing a stir in the media.

Personally, Thomas felt that the longer it dragged on the worse it would be for all those victims and their families involved. According to the papers, video footage had been found which proved that up to a dozen young, vulnerable girls had fallen prey to the accused men. He speculated that this delay would be an extra stress for the Rivers' household, as it would remain hanging over their heads for the near future.

Even though it had been before his time as a Teaching Assistant, Thomas knew that, as a school, they were aware of some of the struggles that Laura had been through over the years. Poppy had been nurtured through the trauma of her dad's death as she had been in her final term of Year Six at Mimosa Primary during that tragic time. The senselessness of it had rocked the community. That unfortunate family were due some luck!

Despite the ominous global situation, the day passed without any major dramas. After lunch, Mrs Redleigh put on a film from her own personal Netflix account; highly illegal but in light of the situation it felt like the seemingly harmless, small misdemeanour was worth it to create a happy, relaxing afternoon for the children. Whilst the class were contentedly sprawled across the tables, engrossed in the plot, the adults tidied the classroom and prepared to empty it of any stray lunchboxes, jumpers and other personal items which seemed to accumulate in the strangest of places.

As they worked, Sophia and Thomas recapped what had been said in the staffroom during lunch break. They whispered across the bookcase as Thomas was half stuck down behind it, headfirst, recovering a missing sock. 'Apparently Boris is going to keep everything shut down 'til the Easter hols!'

'Hmmm, that's not that long though, what will change in a few weeks, Mrs R?'

Shrugging, she took the long grey sock and hauled the TA back to his feet. 'I guess we'll have to just take each day at a time. Some people are saying we will have to wear masks. It will be like something out of a film, you just can't imagine it, can you? Still doesn't seem real!'

They ended the hypothesising as it was almost home time and the children were chivvied into getting their things organised and ready.

Feeling the sense of abnormal occasion, they both went out on to the playground to wave the children off safely, although several would be returning as key worker children after the weekend. A few of the parents stood in small clusters as normal, chatting and catching up. Others stood alone, unsure and wary and almost apologetic about being cautious of standing too close to anyone else. It was a warm, March afternoon but there was a distinct smell of unease and trepidation floating amongst the adults. It seemed to drift onto some of the older children too and lots of hasty farewells were called as cars were scrambled into, faster and more urgently than usual.

Mrs Rose had insisted that all the staff were to leave the premises shortly after the children had left and go home and enjoy the weekend with their loved ones before lockdown officially started on Monday. Hugging Sophia goodbye, after all, they had been working together all day, Thomas wished her well. 'Enjoy working from home on Monday,' he called back down the echoey corridor with a grin. 'You could stay in your pyjamas!'

'Very funny, Mr G,' she retorted, 'I'll be up at the crack of dawn fighting Luke and Ethan for the internet. Luke is going to be attempting to work from home too but is unsure if the company will survive the shut down; I'm sure he will be lovely and stressed and it will be all my fault for having a secure job. Ethan's school have said they will be setting tasks for each subject, so he'll be mutinous and blame me, oh, and I'll probably be chasing after Clara who has just discovered she can run! All sounds joyful! This is before I figure out how to log into the new home learning platform!'

Laughing aloud, but kindly, at the sarcastic deliverance of problems by his eyerolling colleague, he ran back and gave her one last hug and insisted on performing the special hi-five routine that they had made up together, before going to unlock his bike from the Victorian iron railings ready to cycle the few miles home.

Chapter 23

Thomas was up early again on Saturday morning, despite the pounding in his temples from polishing off a whole bottle of white wine the evening before. It had seemed a fitting end to the week, especially when his best friend Kitty had called saying she might be stuck in Australia as all flights were being grounded. He'd missed her since she had been travelling for the last few months and now, it seemed that she was trapped with no money and no way home. His mum had been at work on a night shift so he had been alone in the flat and consequently they had talked and laughed loudly for over an hour, it being early Saturday morning for her. Thomas had unwittingly drunk the entire bottle through the chat. Their call had ended when he had received an email from the supermarket he worked at, asking him to come in at eight o'clock as they were expecting a lot of last-minute panic buyers. After promising Kitty he would investigate flights from the UK end, they had signed off and he had crawled into bed.

Rachel came into the kitchen as he was ironing his work uniform. She was bleary eyed but chirpy as she stood on tiptoe to ruffle his hair. 'Good morning to my favourite son. If you can, please bring some toilet rolls home with you. We only have a couple left and everywhere seems to be out of stock. I did stop at the twenty-four-hour garage on my way back from work earlier, but the shelves there were empty too. It's crazy!' She yawned and reached behind the ironing board to switch on the kettle.

'Guess what?' Rachel looked sheepish as she waited for

Thomas to answer her question.

'Oh God, Mum, what have you done now?' He groaned theatrically and gave her his undivided attention.

'Oh, it's nothing bad, more annoying! Boris' new rules mean neither of us will be able to date for a while, shame really as I was just getting used to all these dating apps you signed me on to. We were talking about it at work. It's gonna be all work and no play for all of us for a while, no social activities. Just you and me hunkered down after work each day, kid! Anyway, I bought some paint – thought we could do the flat up a bit. You game?'

Thomas nodded and flexed his rather poor biceps.

'We've got this, Madre dearest, it'll be an adventure.'

Thomas had never been able to afford to learn to drive but it had never been an issue before between using public transport and riding his bike. Today though, he hesitated at the thought of queuing to board a crowded bus and instead unlocked his bike from the communal bike shed outside the block of four flats. It was almost eight miles to the supermarket but he figured the wind in his hair would blow away any remains of his hangover.

As he finally whizzed through the large carpark, skidding gracefully around the corner, he noticed the vast number of cars and people surging towards the entrance. Grimacing, he dismounted and pushed his bike round to the secluded staff door. The vibe from the shoppers seemed to be like something from an apocalyptic movie. Not much community spirit!

It was a long day and by mid-afternoon Thomas' temples began to throb. In a rare pause between harassed, panicked customers, he took a deep breath and massaged his scalp. He could see things getting heated on the checkout next to his and he watched to make sure his colleague, seventy-year-old Carol was able to manage the situation. Sensing the start of a possible altercation he switched his light off, announcing the closing of his lane, and he went to support Carol, beckoning to Dave the lazy security guard on his way.

'All right, Luvvies? Can I help anyone here?' Thomas addressed the two stressed women who briefly paused in their contemptuous shouting match to glare at him.

The shorter customer pointed to the seven tins of baby milk powder, stacks of nappies and antibacterial wipes in the other woman's trolley. 'She's cleared the shelves! It is selfish and greedy. We all have babies at home that need feeding and keeping clean. It's not right she should take it all!'

The offending woman harrumphed and tried to push past Thomas to continue to Carol's checkout. He could see everyone gathering around. They all looked unsure of the correct protocol. Aware that the shift manager Steve was out the back sorting out a damaged delivery van and its distraught driver, Thomas figured he should probably do something to smooth over the situation.

'Now now, we are all in this together. There is no legal reason why this lovely lady can't buy whatever she likes. It's 2020 and it is her money so let's simmer down, Duckies.' The murmuring crowd had grown. Angry, stressed bystanders were beginning to vocalise their opinions on the situation. The calls from the public to condemn the woman for her selfishness, encouraged by the sight of the desperate, crying mother who had no formula for her own baby who was fast asleep and strapped into the plastic seat of her empty trolley, had grown vindictive towards the shopper.

Thomas turned to where she was trying to shove the items onto the conveyor belt.

'You all right, Chick? Can I help you unload?' The woman glanced around and, swallowing visibly as if she was trying to push back her rogue tears, she nodded haughtily.

He began methodically placing the items ready to be

scanned. Speaking quietly he reassured her it would be okay then he continued, 'You have a whole football team at home? You must do to need all these items in your weekly shop. Twelve packets of nappies!' He was ignored but determinedly carried on, 'Only it's just I've seen you in here before with your husband and son. Heard him say something about you just having moved locally. Beautiful baby you have by the way, but wasn't so keen on the way your husband treated my colleagues, or you for that matter, bit grumpy, isn't he? Anyways, excuse me if I'm speaking out of turn but round here lots of us folk like to look out for each other and we share what we have. Keeps up morale and community spirit and all that. Anyways, excuse my waffling but what I'm trying to say is you look as if you could use a friend or two, especially with your young baby. We don't know what we are going into over these coming weeks, guess it's not the time to be arranging play dates and all that but there's always the phone…'

The woman still hadn't spoken and Thomas had a feeling he was probably going to get sacked today. He had insulted a customer's husband and done nothing to stop the wailing of the mother with the sleeping baby, nor had he pacified the crowd. Carol continued silently scanning the shopping but smiled at him weakly. Glancing behind, he could see Dave half-heartedly disperse the crowd. Most of the onlookers had got bored anyway and had gone back to their own scavenging on the dwindling shelves.

The woman finished paying and gathered up her bags, placing them roughly back in the trolley she hurried towards the exit, head down. The crying woman had abandoned her own trolley and was angrily stomping towards the baby changing room, her now awake child bouncing happily on her hip. The lingering foul smell clarified why she had been so desperate for nappies!

Suddenly, Carol exclaimed loudly and called Thomas over. Left at the end of the packing area was a bag containing two tins of baby milk, two packets of wipes, a large stack of nappies and a bar of chocolate. He grabbed the bag and ran towards the exit. Hopefully he could return it to the woman and apologise too! He found her loading her bags into the boot of a large, older style Volvo. She saw him and froze, her eyes darting towards the driver's seat of the car where Thomas could make out the large figure of a man who was chatting on the phone. Using the raised boot as cover, she gestured towards the trolley bay and Thomas initiatively interpreted the hidden message, and went and waited out of sight of the blue Volvo's occupant.

As she pushed the empty trolley hurriedly towards him, Thomas could see the anxiety written on her face. He held the carrier bag out towards her but the scared looked woman shook her head vigorously. 'It's for her,' she whispered. 'That other lady, I feel bad. I'm not a monster. I was just following orders from his lordship in there…' She nodded back towards the car.

Seeing the front driver's door open. she turned and practically ran back towards the waiting man but Thomas could not un-see the black eye she had tried to cover with her almost immaculate make-up. He hadn't noticed in the store, but in the sunlight it was undeniable.

He wondered what wrath she had risked by leaving the goods behind. Nobody knew what each other person they encountered was going through behind closed doors. What would happen to someone like her and her son whilst they were in lockdown?

Chapter 24

Rachel was at work when Thomas eventually arrived home, having precariously balanced a sought-after packet of nine toilet rolls under his arm whilst he cycled across the fields to take a short cut.

He kicked off his shoes and had just settled down to scroll through his phone whilst semi-watching Saturday night television, when he heard the key turn in the front door and his mum walked in. She looked tired and he instantly sprang up to see if she was all right. It was very unlike Rachel to be sent home when she should be mid shift.

The headache was visible in her eyes as she sank down onto the sofa and closed her eyes. Thomas gave her a cold flannel for her forehead and turned off the overhead light, clicking on the table lamp to give the room a soft, low glow.

'What happened, Mum, you okay?'

'I'll be fine, Tommy. Hopefully I've managed to get home and settled before this pounding beast turns into a killer migraine. The tablets I took before I left work should kick in soon. Be a Love, will you, and fetch me a cold can of something fizzy out of the fridge.'

Rachel kept her eyes shut and tucked her legs up beside her on the sofa, the flannel spread across her face. After she had drunk a few reviving sips of the cold drink, she asked her son to soothe her with his voice, telling her about his day.

'All right, Mummy dearest, you look ever so needy and

pathetic but as I love you dearly, I shall happily oblige.'

He flamboyantly filled her in with avid descriptions of his busy day and the saga of the panic buyers and their desperate attempts of grabbing inconsiderately at non-perishable products. He told the story of what had happened with the two women who both desperately wanted the baby products and he described how the seemingly greedy woman's partner had seemed narcissistic and controlling.

'…So, what happened when you got back in to the store…?'

'The lady was just coming out of the baby changing room. She was ever so grateful. She cried and hugged me. She is also gonna look up the woman on Facebook and invite her to a baby group. Apparently it is going online, like that exercise guy who is going to be doing daily workouts for everyone stuck at home from Monday. Also, it turns out she's the auntie of Ola in my class! Small world as usual. Obviously, Ola speaks highly of me to her entire family!'

Monday dawned brightly. Thomas felt apprehensively surreal as he cycled to Mimosa. The roads were practically deserted and there was an eerie feeling, especially going through the parade of shops, which were all closed with no signs of the normal bustling morning activity. Seeing the shutters of the bakery and the hairdressing salon firmly closed, he shivered involuntarily. It felt apocalyptic!

He was half an hour later than usual. Breakfast club had been cancelled and they were to operate on a shorter timetabled day. Reaching the large, wrought iron gates, he pushed them open and removed his helmet before chaining his bike to the inner railings. Taking a deep breath, he arranged his face into a smile and walked into the building towards the hall, for an impromptu key worker provision briefing.

He needn't have worried. The infectious innocence of the young children soon boosted his spirits. For the next two weeks, he was scheduled to be with the thirteen children that made up the new Year Five and Six bubble. Miss Buzzing, the pastoral school counsellor was his "Teamie" as he called her. They would then both have two weeks at home, monitoring home learning.

The children were a nice bunch, happy to independently get on with the work they had been set. They were to complete the same tasks as the children at home.

As Thomas was thinking about what games they could play outside, to break up the day, he heard his name being called by Arasuli.

'Mr George, please, you help me with this?'

All the other children were dressed in their PE kit that Mrs Rose had declared was the new lockdown uniform, so they would be more comfortable, but Arasuli's had got lost in his sudden house move so he stood out, being the only child in full school uniform, his grey trousers, white shirt and regulation jumper all immaculately ironed. He was having trouble with his Maths task; the 3D shape names unfamiliar to him, even with his new knowledge of English vocabulary.

Thomas sat down next to him and explained each term. Arasuli was a smart, affable boy. He was hungry to learn and grateful for his education. Something that seemed rare these days. He would go far in the future; despite the traumatic experiences he had endured in his young life.

There were no caterers on the school site for lockdown so everyone had brought a packed lunch from home. The two members of staff ate with the children in their bubble – it was lovely to be less formal and more personal with the children, especially when Mrs Redleigh video called and showed them all her new office area she had set up in her living room. They all laughed and cooed when baby Clara appeared in the background, with what looked like nappy cream smeared all over her face and hair. When Mrs Redleigh saw the mess her daughter had got into during the few minutes she had been on the phone, she forgot to hang up the call and they all witnessed her lovingly scoop up her wayward toddler and kiss her on the clean side of her head.

'Mrs Redleigh, Mrs Redleigh,' shouted Ewan, loudly enough that the teacher appeared back on the screen, having retrieved her phone.

Although she looked slightly harassed, they could see her roll her eyes at her squirming daughter, who was now in her arms and rubbing nappy cream on to her cheek. 'Yes, Ewan?'

'You're a good mum and a good teacher. We miss you!'

The call ended abruptly and Thomas secretly wondered if Sophia had ended it deliberately as she had looked a bit emotionally overcome. It must seem really strange for those suddenly stuck at home, trying to be professional and look after their own families at the same time.

After lunch they all spent a long time planning how they would film themselves each day doing dance routines, magic tricks and other sources of entertainment for their teachers and classmates who were at home.

Miss Buzzing quietly reminded Thomas they would have to check that all the children in their care had signed parental consent to be in the videos but they both hoped it would be okay as it would be morale boosting for both those in school and for those at home.

Chapter 25

Otterlie

Otterlie thought that the first week of lockdown had been great! She didn't have to go to school, and even though there was school work to do it was still like an extra holiday! She knew her dad was still going into work; he had to finish the jobs he already had on and then the Government had said he could stay open to help with emergencies for essential vehicles. He had told her that morning that Jim and Stav, who worked for him, weren't allowed to go into the garage under the new rules, so he must do lots of work on his own. Aimee had to close her hairdressing business so she was on school work and child care duty. It had been fun so far. The two of them had begun every day with yoga in the garden then a picnic breakfast on the grass before waking up Elliot. He was panicking as nobody really knew yet what would be happening with his exams. He was getting mixed messages from his teachers and his friends so was being encouraged by his mum to revise a little bit of each subject each day.

Otterlie knew that each time she went past his room, he was just chatting online to his mates and she was not convinced that he was actually doing any school work but as he hadn't been overly mean to her lately, she kept this information to herself!

They spent the mornings sitting at the small kitchen table. Otterlie worked her way through the daily online activities set by Mrs Redleigh. Sometimes there were funny videos to watch too, posted by Mr George and the children in school. Ewan had even attempted a key worker child rap and dedicated it to her. It had been really good and she had written back in the Summer Class discussion thread with lots of emojis. Next week, Mrs Redleigh had promised they could send in clips of themselves playing an instrument or singing at home as part of their lockdown music lesson.

Today, Aimee was standing behind her practicing some elaborate contemporary style on her unruly hair while Otterlie attempted to work out the properties of a sphere. She could not understand if one face was actually the right answer to the faces question, although she had already answered that there were no edges, and, therefore, she was getting a bit fidgety and stressed. Maths confused her brain! The sudden buzz of the doorbell interrupted the scene. Aimee let go of Otterlie's hair to go and answer it. Otterlie crept to the kitchen door to see what was going on. You weren't allowed to visit people's houses, the Government had said so. What if the person had come to contaminate them with the virus?

There did not seem any great need to worry though as it was Mr Gregory, the elderly man who lived next door. He had moved backwards, to keep a safe distance, halfway down the front path and was in a bit of a flustered state, gesticulating wildly. His scruffy green cardigan was buttoned up crookedly and there was dried food on his stained corduroy trousers. Otterlie reckoned he must be about one hundred and fifty years old!

She went and stood next to Aimee and listened to the calm, reassuring voice of her stepmum as she sympathised with the neighbour's woes. Poor Mr Gregory had run out of food over the last week. He was terrified to go to the local shop in case he got ill, besides, he could not walk well enough to get there anyway, let alone carry any produce back, and the bus had stopped running. This meant he had no access to money either as he could not get to the bank to withdraw his pension. He was all alone and starving. It must have taken a great deal of swallowed pride to be standing begging for help, especially for a decorated war veteran.

Luckily, Aimee was a compassionate, warm human being and she instantly took stock and remedied the situation. Otterlie watched in awe as she led the man into the back garden, via the side gate, and sat him on the bench. She disappeared into the kitchen and returned seconds later with a notepad and pen for him to write a shopping list. While he was doing this, painstakingly holding the pen in his shaking hands, Aimee vanished back inside and prepared a chunky cheese sandwich and a cup of tea which she placed on the plastic garden table by his side.

Otterlie sat on the swing, shyly watching. Her wild hair was a halo, framing her face as it was gently ruffled in the spring breeze. She didn't really know what to say to contribute to the conversation. Besides, Mr Gregory did not seem to be able to hear very well as she was on the other side of the garden. The two adults kept a respectful distance from each other too and there was no mention of adjourning inside. The fear of catching or spreading Covid seemed to be at the front of everyone's thoughts, despite the gravity of the situation.

The old man looked so relieved and grateful as he sat back in the sun and slurped his tea. He had finished his list. It only contained essential items; bread, milk, coffee, bacon, cheese, minced lamb, two potatoes, one carrot and a bottle of whisky. As Aimee read it out, to confirm she had deciphered the spidery writing correctly, Otterlie thought to herself that it did not seem to be much food for a week's shop but he seemed satisfied he had not missed anything off.

He finished his sandwich then got shakily to his feet. 'Bless you, my dear, you've been so kind.' His eyes filled with tears but he held Aimee's gaze. 'I'd shake yer hand but that Mr Johnson, up at number ten, says we mustn't.'

'Don't you worry, Mr Gregory; it is no trouble. I will do the online delivery this morning and as soon as it arrives, I will bring it round. In the meantime, you won't starve. We are having a roast chicken tonight and I will plate you up a dinner and pop it over. I will also write my phone number down in case you think of anything else you need. We need to look out for each other in times like this.'

Not attempting to control the tears in his watery eyes that proceeded to slide down his whiskery cheeks, he just smiled gratefully and shuffled back towards his own front door. 'Call me Henry, please. You are the first person I have spoken to for days. At least we should be on first name terms!'

As they ate their meal that evening, Aimee was telling her husband about her good deed. Jonny had seen the crumpled cheque on the kitchen counter that Henry had pressed into her hand with sincere gratitude, when she had taken the steaming plate of roast to his doorstep.

'I can't bring myself to cash it, Jonny. Bless him, he had worked out what he owed to the penny and had the cheque ready for me. I had to anti-bac spray it and wash my hands. Such sad times for a bit of human contact. Anyway, the banks are closed, I think!'

'You're a good egg, Aimee. Remember though we are down to only one income until you know if you qualify for this furlough thing that the chancellor on the news is on about.'

Otterlie lost interest in the conversation and looked at Elliot. He was pushing his peas round on his plate and looking pensive.

She stuck her tongue out at him and smiled but in response she got a hard kick to the shins under the cover of the table.

Otterlie had already been asleep for a few hours but woke up needing to use the toilet. The television was blaring downstairs and judging by the noise it sounded as if her dad and Aimee were watching a scary film. When she walked past Elliot's room, she could hear him animatedly chatting into the headset he was wearing. The invisible people from his computer were obviously goading Elliot as his voice got louder and louder. Angry, defensive tones quivered in his voice. Otterlie hesitated, lingering by his semi-closed bedroom door. Should she see if he was all right? The bruise on her leg chose that moment to throb so she sighed and padded back to her own room, the thick socks she was wearing making no noise on the carpeted landing. Minutes later, from the safety of her bed, she heard a loud, obscene expletive and a bang which sounded like a fist being smashed into the wall.

Jonny ran up the stairs, two at a time, 'What the…? Oh God, look what you've done… Aimee, Aimee?'

Her dad's voice bellowed down the stairs and Aimee could be heard coming out of the kitchen. 'Bring ice!' Jonny shouted down to her then went quickly back into his stepson's bedroom and closed the door. Otterlie had no idea what was going on but it did not sound good!

The following Monday, Otterlie flinched as Aimee threw her phone in anger onto the kitchen sofa, causing Daisy to meow loudly and run out of the room. She had been sitting at the table, engaged in drafting a story about a whale on holiday. Self-sufficient now in the routine of independently getting on with her home learning tasks. Mrs Redleigh was available all morning to help with any queries. They just had to message her through the online platform.

Glancing at her stepmother, she dared ask if everything was all right. Things had been tense since Elliot had severely damaged the wall by putting his fist through it. Her dad had said he could have a few days for the swelling in his knuckles to subside but then he would be expected to pay for the materials and make good the damage. Elliot had been remorseful and had agreed, although he was still very subdued. It had transpired that he had been the victim of horrendous homophobic bullying online. Apparently, it had been going on for months but Elliot had not thought to tell anyone, especially as his own father often belittled him and made him feel inferior because of his sexuality, to the point that Elliot had confessed that he had just thought it was normal, at first.

Thankfully, being in lockdown had ensured that Jonny could not drive to Elliot's father's house and give him a piece of his mind. Thinking back to how her dad had floored the bad men who had tried to grab her, Otterlie thought that her stepbrother's dad had probably had a lucky escape. Her dad was awesome. He hated bullies and put them in their place with his super punches! Aimee sighed. 'That was Elliot's school on the phone. They were not immensely helpful as there is no actual evidence of the threats and the language used as it was either verbal or on social media apps that don't save the conversations. They also said they are waiting for the official Government announcement about exams, they might be cancelled altogether!' Suddenly, realising she was talking to a ten-year-old, Aimee blinked and rubbed her temples. 'You okay to get on with your English work, Love? I need to phone your dad.'

Otterlie quietly did as requested then she went up to her room to practise her song for the class virtual singing performance on Friday. She could see Elliot asleep on his bed, the mid-morning sun blocked out by his closed curtains. So as not to disturb him, she pulled his door closed then firmly shut her own before arranging her favourite teddies to be her adoring audience. Daisy was asleep at the end of her bed so hopefully she would stay and listen too and not wake up and go scatty like she had earlier, hanging off the curtains!

Being grown up seemed so confusing. Why did it matter to anyone else who you wanted to love. Surely it was your own business and didn't hurt anyone else?

As she scrolled through YouTube on her slow, old android tablet, looking for a song to choose, Otterlie decided to be extra nice to Elliot. After all, he had helped her look for her birth mum and he wasn't that bad really. There had been a time a few weeks ago when someone down the street had made a comment about the colour of her skin and Elliot had been straight over to their house to inform the teenager and his parents that there would be consequences if that offensive remark was repeated. He did care about her really!

Even though Ebony would never be in her life, that had been made abundantly clear after the airport saga, Otterlie knew she was lucky to have a great dad and loving stepmum. Her friends were awesome too. Poor Elliot had his mum and Jonny but he also had to deal with a mean dad and rubbish mates. When she had recorded her song, she would make a favourite stepbrother card to cheer him up! Maybe she would even see if he wanted Daisy in his room to make him feel better.

Chapter 26

Bertie

At first, the disruption from his normal life had completely unsettled Bertie, but after a few weeks he had adapted well to the new normal. He was obsessed with the daily briefing from The Prime Minister and watched it religiously, always ensuring they were back from the hour daily exercise slot in time. Now that it was the Easter holidays, he was struggling again. Without the routine of working through the home learning tasks set by school, he had lost his grounding. The days seemed endless to him and boredom was causing Louise to pick on him which added to his agitation.

They often found themselves banished outside, left to their own devices in the vast garden. Luckily the unusually mild April weather had continued and Bertie and his dad had filled the paddling pool the day before. He was languishing in the water when a shadow fell over his eyes.

Louise plonked herself down on the grass with a sigh. She glanced back towards the house before she spoke and even though there was no sign of their parents her voice still came out in a hushed tone, 'Bert, things are not looking good, Dad is in his office upstairs but Mum was crying in the kitchen. I heard them talking, it looks like Dad is going to lose his job. He told Mum he should get some redun… oh I can't remember the word, but anyway some money because he has worked for the company for ten years but he won't have an actual job much longer.'

Bertie held his nose and lay backwards, submerging himself into the chlorinated water. He contemplated the news. It didn't seem that bad. It meant his dad would be at home more with them and if they got hungry, they could always get something from the food bank like Arasuli did. He'd had some really cool sausages and spaghetti in a tin and had told Bertie about it. Counting to ten, he kept his head under the water then suddenly erupted into the air, completely soaking Louise. She shrieked and punched him violently in the back, causing him to gasp. He could hear her wailing as she ran into the kitchen, calling for their mother.

Claudette found him standing by the side of the pool, shivering and in a world of his own. She wrapped him in a large, fluffy, super soft towel and after scooping up his discarded clothes from the wet grass, she led him inside to warm up.

Nobody mentioned the large elephant parading around the dining room as they sat and ate fresh tuna salad for dinner. The only indication that there was anything amiss in the Housten household was the anxious glances and watery smiles the adults kept giving each other as they steadily sipped at their wine. Louise still was not talking to Bertie as he had gotten her favourite teddy wet; apparently, it had been in her pocket! When he had finished eating, Bertie slipped upstairs to his room and immersed himself in the comfort of his large atlas, tracing his fingers over the shape of each country and island. The subconscious tapping of his foot onto the thick, expensive rug calmed him and the feeling of unrest began to dissipate.

Looking at the map made flashes of memory from Arasuli's journey come back. Suddenly feeling the need to speak to his friend, Bertie padded down the stairs to where the home phone was kept on a console table in the long hallway. His dad had left the number next to the phone as promised. He'd told Bertie to call whenever he liked, saying it was important to stay connected with each other during lockdown. Bertie pressed the green button like he'd been shown, but instead of hearing the expected dial tone he could hear his dad's voice loud and clear. He must be on the extension in his office. Unsure what to do, Bertie continued to hold it to his ear. He took two steps backwards and sat on the long wooden bench, practically camouflaged by the leaves which hung low.

'...I know, darling, please don't cry. I can't be held responsible for a global pandemic! I won't make it to Abu Dhabi, I won't make it anywhere. I'm grounded and soon to be unemployed...'

Initially, Bertie thought he was hearing his dad chatting to his mum somewhere else in the house but then a female voice with a heavy French accent cut across the conversation.

'Stephen, you told me it was over with your wife and the twins, I'm all packed ready to move to the UAE with you, start our life together, what are you saying? Actually wait, you are unemployed, what does that mean? How will we afford to start afresh?'

On hearing what sounded like an anguished sob, potentially coming from his father, Bertie dropped the phone as if it had suddenly burst into lava. In his haste to get away and make sense of what he had heard he knocked over the bench and damaged a few stems but he didn't notice. He ran.

It was Louise who found him hours later, long after bedtime. He was curled up asleep under the treehouse's beanbags. The devastation surrounding him proved he had lost control of his emotions and many of the precious items they stored there were upturned or damaged. Waking him gently, she snuggled down next to him.

'What's up, Buttface? Mum's been looking for you to say goodnight.'

Louise's face grew pale in the moonlight as Bertie repeated, word for word, the conversation he had overheard. His voice was monotone but in the still evening it carried clearly enough to the path which Claudette was walking along, looking for her twins.

Nobody was in sight when the children eventually climbed down the sturdy ladder. They had wordlessly done their best to tidy up the mess in the treehouse, making it a safe haven again. Even Louise was speechless which was so unusual that Bertie found it somewhat disconcerting but she punched him affectionately as the entered the kitchen. 'Remember, we can't tell Mum what you heard, not yet.'

The next few days were strained. Stephen announced he was searching for new employment and spent long stretches of the endless days in his office with the door firmly closed. Claudette seemed to be avoiding both the situation and her children. With nowhere to go to escape, she claimed a migraine and rarely left her bedroom. She mostly seemed to live in the same pair of flannel PJs but Stephen was too preoccupied to notice this or the fact that the twins were fending for themselves.

Their perfect, protected world was shattering around them but both Louise and Bertie created their own routine. When a phone call for Louise from Holly broke up their game of Chess, Bertie took a deep breath and went to attempt his own call to Arasuli again.

He panicked a little bit as the line rang in his ear but when Arasuli answered with a "Hi, Bertie" he relaxed. It was so good to hear his friend's voice. He knew that Louise video called Holly and Otterlie but Arasuli only had access to Amir's old phone and it wasn't technically advanced enough for that. Still, a voice call was still good! The boys' call was stilted, although Arasuli was getting much better at the language and was almost fluent now, he'd been at home with his family talking mainly Syrian and his speech had become accented. However, it was Bertie's limited social skills that often stopped each conversation dead. It didn't matter though, both boys were genuinely happy to talk to each other. It was a pleasant distraction from their lockdown home life.

It was Holly who helped get some parental supervision back in the twin's lives. After hearing Louise describe what had been going on she confided in her mum and before long Laura was ringing the doorbell. She had left Holly at home with Poppy and despite Boris' rules, she was now insisting on coming in and demanding Claudette get out of bed.

Bertie looked on in awe as Laura wrinkled up her nose and directed her friend to get in the shower.

'God, Claudette you stink like shit. Where's Stephen?'

Claudette nodded towards the office door and then went off meekly to carry out some much needed personal hygiene as requested. Laura glanced in the kitchen and winced. Taking charge, she called to Louise and Bertie, 'You two – load the dishwasher and wipe over all horizontal surfaces. I'm going to have a chat with your dad and if it's done when I get back, I will order you a Chinese.'

'Er, but we are not allowed takeaway…'

'Today you are,' argued Laura. Leaving the twins to rush to complete the chores, she marched into the office without knocking. Bertie and Louise paused to listen. They could hear the rise and fall of voices but could only make out certain bits. It sounded like their dad was being told off!

They had just finished returning the kitchen to its show home look when Laura appeared with white bags of delicious smelling food.

'You okay, Twinnies?' They both nodded but Louise's worried glance towards the door didn't go unnoticed. Since her own family crisis had made her realise how much her girls relied on her, Laura had been trying really hard to stem her addictions and she was functioning much better. This week was a good week and she had not even had a drink for days. Being needed to be the support for her friend had given her a glow of confidence and she felt good to have a purpose.

'It is okay. Your mum is showered and looking like her old self, your dad has been up to chat with her, but he is going to stay with his brother for a while to give her a bit of time. He knows what you heard, Bertie, and so does your mum. No more secrets, but they both need a bit of space from each other to think things through. Don't worry, we've checked the rules, your dad can go as your uncle lives on his own so they will form a new support bubble.'

Bertie just stood and listened, his left hand rhythmically tapping against his hip but Louise crumpled and began to sob, loudly.

Laura was saved from the dilemma of whether to risk Covid contamination by hugging the child because the door slid open and a composed Claudette appeared, scooping up Louise into her arms. As his mum reached out and drew Bertie into the hug, Laura backed out of the room. 'Enjoy your food treat.'

Bertie watched his mum run after her. 'Thank you so, so much, Laura. Maybe if Catering for Kicks doesn't survive Covid you could take up relationship counselling!'

Just then Stephen came downstairs with a large holdall, the

one he often took on business trips. It all seemed to be happening in slow motion for Bertie. Laura left, closing the front door behind herself, and his dad shakily dumped the bag, walked into the kitchen, and helped himself to a plate of food. It was surreal. The haze he felt was only broken when his dad spoke, 'I love you two so much. I know you both know that I have made some mistakes lately so I am going to stay with Uncle Rob for a while. I need to try everything to prove to your mum I am worth having back. Because of lockdown, I won't be able to come and see you much but I promise to phone every day. First though, can we eat this delicious Chinese food?' Glancing at Claudette, who nodded and shrugged, the four of them perched on bar stools around the kitchen island. It was the first time ever they'd had a takeaway and the first time they had eaten a meal other than breakfast in any room except the dining room.

Surprisingly, Bertie didn't mind. It felt like an important occasion. Besides, he thought the Chow Mein was delicious!

Chapter 27

Holly

Holly winced as Poppy slammed her bedroom door shut. It seemed lockdown was getting to everyone! She sighed and flopped onto her unmade bed. Home learning lessons had finished for the day and she was bored. Poppy had just been in to take the laptop they shared as she had tasks to complete for her college childcare course, but Holly didn't know why her big sister had to be so grumpy.

The court case against the bad men had been postponed until further notice because of the pandemic and in all honesty, Holly knew it was an important thing that would happen in the future but right now it wasn't something constantly on her mind. She guessed it still bothered Poppy and the adults though. She had overheard a phone conversation between her mum and Aimee talking about how unfair that it was stretching past Poppy's seventeenth birthday, meaning she might be expected to stand behind a screen in the main courtroom, to give evidence, rather than be allowed in a separate room via video link.

As Poppy's birthday was the following day, Holly figured this was a sure thing anyway so she did not see the big deal the adults were making about it! Retrieving the homemade card from its hiding place under her bookshelf, Holly chose some of her fine tip felt pens and set about adding colour to finish the drawings she had done for her sister. She was proud of them;

caricatures of their family she had sketched, using a special dark pencil, based on their holiday photos from when they had gone to Wales to visit Grandma and Gramps.

When she had finished, Holly went downstairs to show her mum. Finding her asleep in the conservatory she gently shook her awake, crossing her fingers that she would be greeted with a smile. She was in luck! Laura sat up with a stretch and rubbed her shoulder to restore the blood supply from it being squashed against the wooden arm rest of the hardbacked sofa.

Shyly thrusting her masterpiece in her mum's face, Holly stood back proudly as Laura focused her eyes to look at the card.

'Oh, Holly, this is beautiful. Poppy will love it. Would you like it as a card or shall we frame it? I've seen a lovely wooden one in one of the drawers in my room.'

Holly shrugged so Laura sprang up and rushed to fetch it, knocking over her empty wine glass in her haste. Bending down to pick it up, Holly saw the equally empty bottle which had rolled under the sofa. She collected that too and buried it in the kitchen recycling bin before Poppy saw it and another row erupted between her mum and sister.

Some days Laura would start drinking late morning and steadily fill up her glass throughout the day but there had been times lately that she had stayed sober for days on end, not even joking that it was her vice to get through lockdown. As far as Holly could tell, there didn't seem to be a pattern and it was not hurting anyone. It wasn't like they were going anywhere – some days they did their daily exercise in front of the TV and didn't actually leave the house!

Poppy seemed to like holding it against their mum though. Shouting at her regularly that she was a failure who cared more about oblivion than she did about her daughters. Holly sighed again; she knew that after arguments she was left in the middle. Consoling her mother, who would then take herself off for a guilty cry and usually a comfort glass of wine or instead choosing to go running upstairs to sit with Poppy who would be crying as well, her music full blast and trying to hide her bandaged arms whenever Holly entered the room.

Opening the fridge helped de-stress Holly. Since Poppy had come home from hospital all those months ago, it had never been empty again. It was a promise that had been kept. Helping herself to a fistful of grapes, a chunk of cheese and a couple of chocolate bars she went and sat in the garden to wait for her mum to bring the frame.

Poppy's birthday went well. They decorated the house with balloons and disco lights and the three of them danced and sang karaoke. They had virtual guests drop in throughout the evening. Lots of Poppy's friends were dancing in their own homes in solidarity of a lockdown birthday and Grandma even sang, jubilantly joining in the party spirit but causing them all hysterical laughter when she kept putting the tablet she was holding to her ear, so they just got a view of the side of her head!

Holly took a moment to rest and threw herself onto the brand new comfortable light blue corner sofa in the front room. Rufus appeared from under the curtains where he had been hiding in the excitement and suddenly shot across her lap and out the door, scratching her arm on the way. Laura had chosen that moment to pop to the toilet but Poppy noticed her tears and flopped next to her, pulling her into a hug. 'You'll be okay, Hols, it has hardly broken the skin, I'll get you some wet kitchen roll. Thank you again for my present, I love it so much.'

When Poppy returned, handing her the wet compress, Holly

held it on her cat scratch and looked at her sister. 'Did the cats scratch you too, Pops? Is that why you have bandages on your arms. Are they sore like mine?'

The birthday girl yanked down the sleeves of her dress and looked at her young, innocent sister. 'Er, yes, Hols. Silly cats. Please don't tell Mum though, I don't want her to worry that the cats are dangerous, in case we have to get rid of them.'

The thought of losing the beloved cats made Holly agree straight away to keep the secret. That worrisome feeling squirmed in her stomach though. Holly wasn't one hundred percent sure why.

The party continued into the night. Laura was relaxed and having a wonderful time, twirling both girls around the living room with bright eyes and a big smile. She pretended not to notice when Poppy swiped an open bottle of wine from the coffee table and helped herself, drinking thirstily from the bottle. Holly watched and smiled. She loved her family.

After the weekend, they settled back into a routine. Even though Laura had been forced to close her business, they would never be short of money. Marcus had set up a very comprehensive life insurance policy before he died which provided a generous monthly income, plus it had paid off the mortgage.

The new laptop that Laura had ordered arrived and was given to Poppy so both girls could now sit and do their required home learning without having to share. Laura was at the rustic kitchen table with Holly, helping her with her work but also browsing through catering magazines which had been delivered too that morning. They religiously sprayed each package with antibacterial solution before opening them. Same as each item when the weekly food shopping was delivered. Mrs Redleigh had set a Maths task which was to finish up their prior learning with a test of what they knew about word problems. Holly was chewing the end of her pen while she thought about how to answer the three-step question when Laura's mobile rang. It was Claudette.

Pretending to be absorbed in her school work, Holly was really straining her ears to hear the adult conversation. She knew that Louise's dad had moved out a few weeks ago but now it seemed that Claudette had decided to forgive him and they were going to use lockdown to spend quality time at home as a family and try and work things out. They had enough savings to have a month or two without Stephen's income but it wasn't like they could go anywhere to spend any money like they usually did…

Holly got bored with the financial chat and stopped listening. She was proud of herself for independently getting on with her work so she messaged the Summer Class discussion chat to let Mrs Redleigh know she had completed the Maths test and would upload it. Otterlie wrote something on the chat thread too and the two of them started an online emoji competition until they were reprimanded by Mrs Redleigh, who reminded them the chat was for helpful hints to each other about the school work. Feeling brave, Holly replied to the teacher, asking why Mr George hadn't uploaded the fun things the key worker children had been up to. She was told in reply that it wasn't Mr George's week to be on the school rota.

Later, when Otterlie called Holly, they discussed this. Otterlie told her that she had seen Ewan when he walked past her front garden on the way home from school and they'd had a quick chat, calling across the fence to keep apart. According to Ewan, Mr George's mum had caught Covid-19 when it had spread through the nursing home she worked at. Several of the residents had been taken to hospital and two had sadly died. Callum's mum worked at the hospital and when Callum had overheard this information between his parents, he had told Joe and Ewan, who had then told Otterlie.

Holly and Otterlie concluded that Mr George was not at school because he had been looking after his mum. They didn't dwell on the subject for long though because more exciting was the news from the Government Team that schools were not going to be fully opened until after the summer holidays! They still had to continue with home learning until the end of term but it wasn't so bad. They could chat in the forum and send each other videos. Even Arasuli had got the hang of it and was becoming more and more confident with showing everyone his art work. He had decorated the walls of his dreary accommodation with vibrant, bold colours and patterns.

Chapter 28

Thomas

Thomas was disorientated but vaguely aware of his surroundings. He knew that he was in hospital but he weirdly seemed to be floating, dazed, most of the time. The memory of an ambulance ride, with the paramedics telling his sick mum to stay home, plagued his semi-lucid dreams. Sometimes, over the last few vague hours/days he had felt like he was outside a steamed-up window, watching some guy who looked like a haggard version of himself lying in a ward with equally sick-looking, forlorn and desperate companions around him. Other times, it was definitely him, physically present in the narrow bed, gasping to catch an extremely painful but precious breath. A rhino seemed to be compressing his chest, disabling his lungs so they could not inflate and fill properly. Voices swam around him, talking about foreign concepts such as, '…needs to be fully ventilated, Obs not great, next of kin is positive too…' Alien-like creatures in white suits, gloves, masks, and visors, with only fatigued, human eyes visible, spoke soothingly near his ears but he could not form the words aloud to reply. If breathing was too difficult, it made talking impossible. It was better when the bright strip lights faded and the darkness swarmed, cushioning him…